Praise for th

"Daley's characters come to life on the page. Her novels are filled with a little mystery and a little romance which makes for a murderous adventure."

– Tonya Kappes,
USA Today Bestselling Author of *Fixin' To Die*

"Daley's mysteries offer as much sizzle and pop as fireworks on a hot summer's day."

– Mary Kennedy,
Author of The Dream Club Mysteries

"I'm a huge fan of Kathi's books. I think I've read every one. Without a doubt, she's a gifted cozy mystery author and I eagerly await each new release!"

– Dianne Harman,
Author of the High Desert Cozy Mysteries

"Intriguing, likeable characters, keep-you-guessing mysteries, and settings that literally transport you to Paradise...Daley's stories draw you in and keep you glued until the very last page."

– Tracy Weber,
Agatha-Nominated Author of the Downward Dog Mysteries

"Daley really knows how to write a top-notch cozy."

– *MJB Reviewers*

"Kathi Daley writes a story with a puzzling cold-case mystery while highlighting...the love of home, family, and good friends."

– *Chatting About Cozies*

Halloween
IN
PARADISE

**The Tj Jensen Mystery Series
by Kathi Daley**

Halloween

A TJ JENSEN MYSTERY

IN PARADISE

KATHI DALEY

HENERY PRESS

ᴵN IN PARADISE
ᴶen Mystery
ᴬʳt of the Henery Press Mystery Collection

Second Edition | September 2016

Henery Press, LLC
www.henerypress.com

Trade Paperback ISBN-13: 978-1-63511-109-5
Digital epub ISBN-13: 978-1-63511-110-1
Kindle ISBN-13: 978-1-63511-111-8
Hardcover Paperback ISBN-13: 978-1-63511-112-5

Printed in the United States of America

This book is dedicated to my Halloween loving grandchildren: Isaiah, Eisley, Maleia, Greyson, and Maevelynn.

ACKNOWLEDGMENTS

They say it takes a village and I have a great one.

I want to thank all my friends who hang out over at my Kathi Daley Books Group page on Facebook. This exceptional group help me not only with promotion but with helpful suggestion and feedback as well.

I want to thank the bloggers who have pretty much adopted me and have helped me to build a fantastic social media presence. There are too many to list, but I want to specifically recognize Dru Ann Love for her expert guidance and support.

I want to thank my fellow authors who I run to all the time when I don't know how to do something or how to deal with a situation. I have to say that the cozy mystery family is about as close-knit a family as you are likely to find anywhere.

I want to thank Bruce Curran for generously helping me with all my techy questions and Ricky Turner for help with my webpage.

I want to thank my graphic designer Jessica Fisher for all my flashy ads and headers.

I want to thank Randy Ladenheim-Gil for making what I write legible.

I want to thank Art Molinares for welcoming me so enthusiastically to the Henery Press family and a special thank you to Erin George and the entire editing crew who have been so incredibly awesome and fun to work with.

And last but certainly not least, I want to thank my super-husband Ken for allowing me time to write by taking care of everything else (and I mean everything).

CHAPTER 1

Monday, October 26

"Coach Jensen." Carly Rice, one of the juniors on Tj Jensen's soccer team, poked her head through her office door. "You wanted to see me?"

"I did. Please have a seat." Tj motioned to the only surface in her cluttered office that wasn't covered with file folders or athletic equipment. As chairperson for the department, it was her responsibility to apply for grants and file reports, two jobs she could never seem to find time to do, despite the extra prep period she was granted for just that purpose.

Carly sat down as instructed. "Am I being suspended from the team?" she asked sullenly.

"You know I have no other choice," Tj said with sympathy in her eyes. "If I could do things differently I would."

Carly was the best forward Tj had on her team. She really

did feel bad that it had come to this. Not only would Carly's suspension hurt the junior herself, but it would hurt the team's chances of making it to the state finals.

Tj had worked with many talented kids during her tenure as a coach and physical education teacher, and few exhibited the drive to compete and win that Carly did. Or at least she had until her world crumbled around her and everything changed.

Carly sighed. "I guess I'll kiss any chance at a scholarship goodbye, which means I won't be able to go to college or get a decent job. I may as well pick out a box to live in and get on with my life."

Tj suppressed a smile. Carly really did have a flare for the dramatic. "I don't think things are quite that dire. You're still a junior, so you have time to redeem yourself, especially if you take on a new attitude. But if you don't learn to control your temper, you won't be allowed to try out for the team next year. Soccer isn't football. You can't just tackle people in your way."

"I know. I just get so mad. Someone gets in front of me and the only thing I can think of is how much I want to flatten them."

And flatten them she did. Carly was a tiny thing, but she could take down her opponents as effectively as any linebacker. She'd let Carly's bad behavior in class and on the soccer field slide as long as she could, but after she'd intentionally tackled an opposing team member then elbowed her in the stomach, Tj realized she had no choice but to suspend her.

"I understand you've had it rough," Tj said. "I can't imagine how awful it must be to lose a brother. You're angry and need an outlet for your emotion, but the league has very strict rules regarding intentional roughhousing."

"I know."

"Have you considered counseling?" Tj asked. This wasn't the first time that Tj had tried to persuade Carly to seek counseling after the death of her brother the prior summer.

Carly glared at her with dark brown eyes filled with pain. "My brother died. I'm angry about *that*," she emphasized as she tucked a lock of her long brown hair behind one ear. She was fighting back tears as she spoke. "I'm not a nutcase who needs to see a shrink."

"I never said you were a nutcase. I'm not an expert on the subject, but I've heard there are wonderful counselors who can help you work through the feelings you've been dealing with since Kenny was killed. I know I've suggested this before, but maybe you should speak to Mrs. Remington."

Sheila Remington was the school counselor.

Carly looked Tj directly in the eye. "You think she can help me? You think *anyone* can help me? You have no idea what it's like to be the child who didn't die. To be the child who knows deep in her heart that her mom—and everyone else, for that matter—wishes she was the twin who died and Kenny was the one who lived?"

"I'm sure your mom doesn't think that."

"You don't know. You don't know anything," Carly yelled. "My mom *hates* me. Every time she looks at me, I can see it in her eyes. If I hadn't forgotten to check in while I was out with my friends, Kenny wouldn't have come looking for me, and if Kenny hadn't been out looking for me, he wouldn't have been riding his bike on the street, and if he hadn't been riding on the street, he wouldn't have been hit by a car.

Kenny is dead and it's my fault. I know it, my mom knows it, everyone knows it. Even my friends don't want to hang out with me anymore."

Tj suspected Carly's friends were avoiding her due to the chip on her shoulder causing world-class mood swings and violent outbursts, not because they blamed her for Kenny's death. Still, Kenny had been popular. Really popular. He was the star of both the football and baseball teams, and prior to his death, he'd been dating Portia Waldron, the most popular girl in the junior class. Portia could very well have blackballed Carly from their social circle. Tj hated to think the girl would do such a thing, but she'd been around long enough to know that kids could be cruel.

Tj struggled for the right thing to say. She hated to leave it like this, but as hard as she tried, her brain refused to formulate words that might prove helpful in this situation.

"If that's all, I need to go. I have class." Carly stood up. "Not that it will matter if I'm late because I'm flunking anyway, but I suppose I have to go somewhere. It might as well be class."

"Carly." Tj attempted to stop Carly from leaving, but the girl didn't look back as she slammed the door behind her.

Tj let out a groan. That certainly hadn't gone as she'd hoped. She wanted to help Carly, but she was in over her head with this one. Carly needed professional help she wasn't qualified to give. She'd talked to Carly's mother about it, but the mom had been unresponsive. Tj knew the woman had all but shut down since Kenny's death, but Carly needed someone to help her work through her grief and get on with her life.

"I take it your talk with Carly didn't go well?" Gina

Roberts, the new math teacher, poked her head into Tj's office shortly after Carly stormed off.

"Not even close. If it was possible to make things worse I think I just did."

Gina left the door open as she walked into the office and took a seat on the other side of Tj's desk. "The girl needs professional help."

Tj agreed. "The problem is, she's totally closed off to the idea, and her mother doesn't seem willing to pursue it. I wish I could force the issue, but I don't have any grounds to do so. Carly is self-destructive, but other than being overly aggressive on the soccer field, she hasn't hurt anyone, and I can't honestly say I think she'll seriously hurt herself. If I thought calling child services would help I might consider it, but to be honest, I think that would just make things worse. Carly is a good kid. I really believe she can work her way through this if she'll just forgive herself. At this point, I don't think she believes she deserves any of the good things in life that she's worked so hard to achieve. It's almost like she's punishing herself by creating situations where she knows she'll lose things that were previously important to her."

"Don't give up on her," Gina counseled. "I can see she wants to open up to you. Part of me thinks she acts the way she does to get your attention. I haven't spoken to her mother, but I've heard through the rumor mill in the teachers' lounge that there are staff members who have tried with zero success to get her mom to agree to counseling. I can't imagine why she's pushing away her only remaining child, but then again I have no children, so what do I know? Carly likes and respects you. In my opinion, you may very well be the only person who can help her."

"Maybe, but I had to suspend her from the soccer team for the rest of the season after the incident this weekend. It's going to hurt her shot at a scholarship, and her removal from the team means I'll be seeing much less of her."

"Make her an assistant," Gina suggested. "I'd be willing to bet a whole paycheck that if you asked her to help you out she would."

Tj considered the idea. "I'll think about it. I don't want it to seem like I'm rewarding her bad behavior, but I might be able to work it out so that her helping me appears to be punishment to the other girls. Thanks for the suggestion."

"Anytime. But I actually came by to talk about another student we have in common."

"Lexi Michaels," Tj guessed. "I was just checking my email and saw the video. Do we know who sent it?"

Lexi Michaels was another of Tj's soccer girls. The poor kid had recently become Serenity High School's latest cyberbullying victim when someone posted a video of her singing in the locker room while showering after practice the night before. According to Gina, Lexi thought she was alone in the locker room, but apparently there had been at least one other straggler who had taken it upon herself to record the revealing and unflattering karaoke session and then post it online for everyone to see.

"The video was posted from a burner cell, so there's no way to trace it back to a specific student," Gina said. "I spoke to Lexi, who is quite predictably horrified. She went home halfway through my class, and I'm not sure she'll be back tomorrow. We were able to have the video taken down but I'm afraid the damage has been done. The poor girl is devastated."

Tj shook her head. With the advent of social media and the tendency for teens to use it as a weapon, cyberbullying had become an increasingly serious issue at the school.

"I'll do some snooping to see if I can figure out who posted the video," Tj offered. "If it happened after soccer practice it was probably one of my girls. I'll figure out who did this and make sure they're punished accordingly." Tj looked at her watch. "I guess we should get to the staff meeting."

"Didn't you hear? This afternoon's meeting was canceled. I was in the admin office earlier and ran into Principal Remington. He's going to be tied up with Lexi's mom all afternoon. I bet there's a note on the message board by now."

"Actually that works out well for me. I have a ton of paperwork to weed through."

Gina looked around the office and laughed. "I'm not sure that an extra couple of hours is even going to make a dent but it's a start. Is there anything I can help you with?"

"Do you know anything about grant proposals?"

Gina shrugged. "I've written a few."

"I'm currently working on two. If you have some spare time and want to help me I would be very grateful."

"I have time this weekend."

"I have my ten-year reunion this weekend. Maybe next week?"

"Sure just let me know. One of the tricks I've learned over the years is to..."

"Coach Jensen, you have a call on line one," the student aide announced over the intercom interrupting their conversation.

Tj glanced at the phone.

"Go ahead. It might be important."

"Coach Jensen," Tj greeted as she picked up the phone.

"Hey, Tj. It's Roy." Roy Fisher was the deputy sheriff who served the Serenity branch of the Paradise County Sheriff's Department.

"Hey, Roy. Why didn't you just call my cell?"

"I tried to, but you didn't pick up. This is kind of important, so I decided to call the school line. I figured if you weren't in your office I could at least be certain you'd get a message."

"What's wrong?" Tj asked with a tone of dread in her voice. Roy calling her at work was never a good sign.

"Samantha Colton."

"Who's Samantha Colton?" Tj asked.

"She's one of the investigators on *Second Look*."

"*Second Look* as in the show that investigates cold cases and then airs their findings on television?"

"That's the one. She'll be in town tomorrow, taking a 'second look' at Holly Riverton's murder. She wants to talk to everyone who was at the party the night Holly died, including you."

"I'm happy to talk to her, and you know I'm always happy to help you out, but I'm really swamped this week."

"I arranged for her to come to you," Roy informed her. "She's going to stop by the school tomorrow during your prep, so it shouldn't interrupt your day in the least."

"Oh, okay. I'd planned to grade midterms then, but I can take them home and tackle them tonight."

"I appreciate your meeting with her. There's one thing you should be aware of, though. She's known for being aggressive in her bid to find the truth. Anyone who might have a secret of any sort should be prepared to have it revealed."

Tj glanced at Gina and frowned. "What do you mean by *aggressive?*"

Roy sighed. Tj could tell he was feeling uncomfortable about asking her to meet with the woman, but apparently he had little choice but to cooperate.

"She does her homework and it seems like she sees a motive in almost every situation. She's good at what she does. I think you're her first appointment in this area, but she stopped off in Los Angeles yesterday and spoke to Mia Monroe and Jada Jenkins. Both women called me in a rage and indicated they no longer plan to attend the homecoming reunion this weekend."

"What could this woman possibly have said to convince them to change their plans at the last minute?"

"I think it's more how she said it and what her comments implied. Do you remember Mia as being passive-aggressive in high school?" Roy asked.

Tj sat back in her chair as she thought about it. Mia definitely tended to march to the beat of her own drum, but passive-aggressive? "Not really. She was always very self-confident. A drama geek who had no use for the popular kids, like she thought herself to be above their crowd. Though a lot of those kids still made fun of the way she dressed and her odd interests."

"Odd interests?"

"She was really into supernatural stuff like astrology and past lives. And she liked to dress in loud colors. I'm talking bright green pants paired with a hot pink t-shirt topped with blue hair. She also tended to do things she knew would invite ridicule. I think she liked the negative attention."

"What kind of things?" Roy asked.

Tj smiled as she remembered some of Mia's theatrics. "Sometimes she would stand up on one of the tables in the lunch room and start reciting Shakespeare. Or other times, she'd sing at the top of her lungs while she walked through the hallways on her way to class. She certainly wasn't afraid to call attention to herself, which I guess partially explains why she's been so incredibly successful as an actress. What did Colton say that made Mia so mad?"

"Ms. Colton indicated that, given her profile, Mia made an excellent suspect in Holly's murder case."

"What?" Tj glanced at Gina who was hanging on every word of the one sided conversation she was witnessing. "Why would Mia kill Holly?"

"Ms. Colton seems to think Mia was jealous of Holly's popularity and killed her in some sort of psychotic rage. Or at least that's what Mia said. I suspect she might've embellished Ms. Colton's words just a bit."

"That's crazy. Mia never seemed like the type to be jealous of anyone. In fact, based on what I remember, I don't think she cared what people thought of her at all. And Jada, she was one of the most straight-laced girls in our class. I can't imagine what she dug up on her."

"Ms. Colton has reason to believe that Jada cheated on her mid-term exams."

"There's no way. Jada was one of the smartest kids in my class. She didn't need to cheat."

"Ms. Colton shared with me that she believes Holly somehow found out Jada cheated and threatened to tell the administration unless she used her tech know-how to break into the email accounts of some of her fellow students."

"Why would Holly want the email accounts of her fellow students?"

"Ms. Colton didn't say."

"This Samantha Colton sounds like a real piece of work. Are you sure I need to meet with her?"

"I can't force you to, but it will make it look like you have something to hide if you don't. The woman's on a witch hunt, and I don't think she's leaving without her killer."

"Why exactly was the killer never caught?" Tj asked.

"I'm not sure. After Ms. Colton called I took a look at the original file. It looks like there was an adequate if not inspired investigation into the girl's death, due mostly I suspect, to the fact that the Serenity branch of the Paradise County Sheriff's department was in disarray."

"Disarray?"

"There had been a turnover in personnel due to retirement and injury and the Serenity office was being staffed by temporary deputies from Indulgence." Indulgence, with its casinos and five-star dining and lodging, was much larger than Serenity and served as the Paradise County seat.

"I guess the Serenity office was the stepchild of Paradise County even back then." A year ago there had been three deputies permanently assigned to the Serenity office, but Roy had been handling things on his own with the assistance of temps from the Indulgence office since Deputy Dylan Caine resigned and Deputy Tim Matthews was arrested.

"It does seem like the Serenity office is understaffed much of the time," Roy sighed. "Although Sheriff Boggs has promised to assign a full-time deputy to the Serenity office before ski season kicks in. Anyway, as for the investigation, twenty people were interviewed but the deputies who were in charge of the initial investigation only managed to narrow the list down to eight."

"Will you be around if I come by after school lets out?"

"I can be, unless I'm called out."

"If I can get someone to watch the girls for a bit, I'd like to come by and go over the old report with you before my meeting with Ms. Colton."

"Okay. Sounds good. I'll see you then."

"Sorry," Tj said to Gina after hanging up. "I had no idea that would take so long."

"What was that all about?"

"Ten years ago, on the night of the homecoming dance, a girl named Holly Riverton was murdered after attending a party at the star quarterback's home. Her body was found the next morning in the woods near the guy's house. She'd been hit over the head and left to die. The killer was never caught so now someone from *Second Look* is here to take a second look."

"I've seen that show. They do a good job and more often than not find their killer but why are they looking into it now?"

"As I mentioned, it's our ten-year reunion and a lot of the people who were at the party where Holly was killed will be here. I guess the *Second Look* folks thought this would be a good opportunity."

Gina sat forward in her chair. She tucked a lock of her short brown hair behind her ear. Her eyes flashed with curiosity as she asked, "Do you have a theory as to what might have happened?"

"Honestly? No. It's odd, but I really haven't thought about it all that much since it first happened. You know how it is once you graduate. High school, and incidences associated with high school, become but a distant memory once you leave for college."

"I heard you mention Mia to Roy. Were you talking about Mia Monroe the actress?"

"Yeah, although back then she was just Mia Monroe the drama geek with an attitude."

"Wow. I don't think we had anyone famous in my graduating class."

"There were actually several very successful people in my class. Jada Jenkins was a computer geek in high school, but she went on to develop some software and is now a multimillionaire. Brett Conrad played professional football until he was injured and now he is a sportscaster. Jessie Baldwin skied in the Olympics, and another friend, our class valedictorian, Mackenzie Paulson works for NASA as some sort of high-tech scientist. And of course there is Nathan Fullerton."

Gina's eyes looked like they doubled in size. "The writer?"

"One and the same." When Tj was in high school, Nathan had been the editor of the school newspaper. He'd been a talented student who went on to become a *New York Times* bestselling author.

"Do you think he'll be at the reunion?"

"He is going to be there," Tj confirmed. "My grandpa's friend Bookman knows him, so he invited him to stay at his house. I'm pretty sure he's already in town. My grandpa mentioned something about meeting him when he went to his regular poker game at Bookman's last weekend. I remember Nathan being sort of stoic. It'll be fun to see if fame has changed him."

"Wow. I love him. His writing is so real; so emotionally seductive. Any chance you can introduce us?"

"Sure. If the opportunity presents itself."

Tj had to admit that Gina looked about as excited as she'd ever seen her. Nathan was fairly famous in addition to being a babe. She guessed she understood Gina's fascination.

"Is Nathan a suspect in the case?" Gina asked.

"Everyone at the party was considered to be a suspect at the time of the murder. I'm not sure who the *Second Look* reporter plans to interview at this point."

"Do any of the original suspects still live in Serenity?"

"A few. If you define a suspect as anyone who was at the party."

This really seemed to grab Gina's interest. "Like who?"

"I was there with Hunter, Jenna and Dennis Elston were there, Doreen Sullwold, Dalton Fowler, and Teddy Bolton were all there as well."

"Teddy Bolton the dentist?"

"Yeah, although it seems he was cleared during the first investigation along with Jenna and Dennis who left early, and Jim Hanover, who was only at the party for a few minutes."

A look of doubt crossed Gina's face. "As in the Jim Hanover who currently teaches at Serenity High School? I can't imagine stodgy Jim attending a student party."

"He was different back then. I know he's uptight and rigid now, but he was a fun guy when he first started teaching. He could often be found hanging out with the students, and he definitely was the teacher to go to if you had a problcm."

Gina giggled. "It's so weird to try to picture him in the young-and-cool-teacher role."

"He's changed a lot in the past ten years," Tj admitted

The first bell, notifying the physical education classes to head into the locker rooms, sounded in the distance. Tj knew that in a few minutes the hallway would be filled with students. She began setting files aside and turning things off.

"While this is all terribly fascinating, I guess I should get going," Gina stood up. "Let me know if you come up with an idea to help Lexi. In the meantime, I'll see if I can come up with something as well."

CHAPTER 2

Every year Tj vowed to get an earlier start on holiday planning and preparation, but every year she found herself running around trying to get things done at the last minute. She'd hoped that fulfilling the mother role for her sisters would get easier as time went by, but so far it was as hard as it had ever been to fit so many pieces into her totally overloaded life.

"I thought we were going to study hall after school because you had a meeting," redheaded, green-eyed Ashley greeted as Tj hurried toward her.

"Change of plan. Grab your stuff and let's hurry to see if we can catch Gracie before she leaves her classroom."

"She's always the last one out," Ashley reminded her. "I don't think you have to worry. Can we go to a movie tonight?"

"*The Great Pumpkin* is on television tonight."

"*The Great Pumpkin* is for babies."

"No it's not. I love *The Great Pumpkin*," Tj countered, "and I'm a long way from being a baby."

"Me and Kristi want to go to the Halloween movie marathon over at the fourplex," Ashley announced.

"The Halloween marathon is playing horror movies," Tj pointed out as she transferred the pile of tests she'd brought home to grade from one arm to the other. "I'm not sure the movies they're featuring are appropriate for your age group."

"I'm in the fifth grade. I'm not afraid of scary movies and I'm not a baby," Ashley argued. "If we can't go tonight, can I go this weekend? Everyone in my class is going to be there then."

"I doubt everyone in your class is going."

"You are so overprotective." Ashley groaned. "Mom would have let me go."

"We've talked about this before," Tj reminded her sister as they hurried through the crowded hallway. "I'm not Mom and I'm not going to make every decision the way she would have. Still, the movie marathon does sound exactly like something I would have been dying to go to when I was your age, so how about if I check out the lineup and talk to Jenna and then let you know?"

"Okay, but do it soon. You always say you're going to do things, but then you get busy and forget to do them."

"No, I don't. I'm very good about following through."

"No, you're not. You think you are, but you're not."

Tj sighed. She knew it would do her no good to argue with her sister. It was hard to walk the line between being a mother and a sister. If Ashley was actually her daughter, she'd never let her sass her the way she tended to do. On the other hand, Tj knew sisters argued and sassed one another all the time.

"I'll talk to Jenna this afternoon," Tj assured Ashley as they rounded the corner to the hallway where the second grade classes were held. "I promise."

"Tj!" Gracie squealed as she ran into her arms. "Did you get off early?"

"I did."

Gracie gave Tj a kiss on her cheek after wrapping her arms around her neck.

"Go grab your stuff," Tj instructed.

Gracie ran back toward the cubbies where the students kept their personal belongings. After Tj confirmed she had everything she needed, the trio headed down the hall to the parking lot shared by both the elementary and the high school.

It was a beautiful autumn afternoon. The trees lining the front walk of the school were a brilliant gold and a gentle breeze created a melody that reminded Tj why the trees were called quaking aspens. Ashley kicked at the leaves as they walked while Gracie chatted about this and that as she clung to Tj's hand.

When they arrived at the 4Runner, Tj set the paperwork she'd been holding on the passenger seat of the vehicle before walking around to the opposite side. She buckled her sisters in then slid into the driver's seat.

She said a silent prayer that her ancient vehicle would start and then turned the key. When the engine roared right away, she sighed in relief. She really did need to get a new car, but she was attached to the one she'd had since she'd first learned to drive.

"How was school?" Tj asked.

"Boring," Ashley answered.

"I thought you liked school."

"I did. But now it's boring. The teacher keeps going over stuff we already learned."

Ashley was an exceptionally bright student who really should be in gifted classes, but so far Tj had been unsuccessful in getting her to agree to take the placement test. Ashley insisted she wanted to be in the normal class with her friends and not the special one with all the geeky kids. Tj understood that a stable social environment was important for Ashley so she didn't force the issue, but she was concerned Ashley would become so bored she'd stop trying.

"Did you ask your teacher about doing extra credit work during those times she feels the need to review for the other students," Tj asked.

"No. Extra credit is just extra work."

Tj supposed Ashley had a point.

"Maybe you can bring a book and keep it in your desk," Tj suggested. "That way if you get bored you can read quietly so you aren't disturbing the other students."

"Maybe. It still sounds like extra work, though."

"I made the finals for the spelling bee," Gracie announced. "That's extra work, but it's also fun."

"Congratulations. That's wonderful," Tj praised. "When are the finals?"

"The school finals are on Thursday, and then the winner of that round in each group goes on to the regional finals, which are in Carson City. I'm going to study really hard 'cause I think it would be fun to go to Carson City."

"That *would* be fun," Tj agreed. "I'll help you study. I'm sure Grandpa and Papa will as well."

"I have a list of words to learn. I already know most of them because they're from the list I've been studying, but they added some for the final round and there are a few I get mixed up on."

"We'll work on them tonight after dinner. Right now I have a bunch of errands to take care of before we head home."

"Like shopping for costumes?" Ashley asked.

"Like shopping for costumes." Tj agreed. "But I also need to go and talk to Deputy Fisher. I'm going to drop you at The Antiquery," Tj referred to the café/antique shop her best friend Jenna owned along with her mother Helen. "Jenna will give you a snack and then after I get back from the sheriff's office we will go to the costume store."

After dropping the girls off and chatting with Jenna for a few minutes Tj headed to the sheriff's office. It seemed to Tj that the main office didn't take the Serenity office as seriously as it should, and it was a fact that the Serenity office was really just a tiny building with a single jail cell and a couple of offices. When Tj arrived Roy was sitting in the reception area working on one of the computers.

"Thank you for taking the time to meet with me," Tj greeted.

"I'm always happy to. It seems like lately you've done more to solve crime around here than the men and women who are paid to do the job."

"So about the original report." Tj had a ton of errands to do so it was best to get right to the point.

"Like I said. The Serenity office was being manned by temps from the main office at the time of the murder. Two men were assigned to the case neither of which still work for the county. I can probably track them down if we feel at some point that doing so would be helpful, but at this point I'm planning to let the report stand on its own and see what develops. I'm hoping we can get a better feel for what the

Second Look folks are focusing on once Samantha Colton blows into town."

"You said twenty people were interviewed during the initial investigation."

"According to this." Roy handed Tj the report. Roy was correct. According to the report there had been twenty people interviewed, and all twenty people had been at the party on the night Holly died. While Tj agreed that the killer had most likely attended the party, the murder did happen in the woods behind the house and not inside the house. It was shortsighted not to have at least considered any other scenarios.

"Of the twenty it looks like everyone was cleared except for eight people," Roy continued while Tj read. "Brett Conrad, Jessie Baldwin, Mackenzie Paulson, Nathan Fullerton, Mia Monroe, Jada Jenkins, Dalton Fowler, and you."

"Yes, I confess. I did it." Tj laughed.

"I know that most of the people on this list are not viable suspects but I guess I can understand why *Second Look* might be interested in the case. There are a lot of stones that were left unturned during the initial investigation."

"I have to agree. I'm not sure how the other interviews went but I do remember mine. One of the loaner deputies came to my home and asked me a bunch of questions about who Holly had been hanging out with and who might have motive to want her dead. It's interesting that I wasn't cleared. I don't remember saying anything incriminating, and I both came to and left from the party with Hunter and he is cleared. Weird."

"I seem to remember that there was talk at the time that you were jealous that Holly made homecoming queen and you hadn't. There was even some talk that you accused her of cheating."

Tj laughed. "Well yeah, there was that. And she did cheat I just couldn't prove it. But I promise I wouldn't have killed her over our rivalry."

"I know that but the men who investigated the case didn't know you like I do. If I were you I'd be prepared for Ms. Colton to ask you about the controversy which resulted from the homecoming vote."

"Yeah, I will."

Tj looked down at the list. The party had been held at Brett Conrad's home and it was well known that he didn't get along with Holly, so it made sense he was a key suspect. Jessie Baldwin was Holly's best friend. It did seem odd that she was on the list. Tj didn't remember there being any real problems between Holly and Jessie. In fact, if anything they seemed oddly close.

Tj had no idea why Mackenzie Paulson, Nathan Fullerton, Mia Monroe, or Jada Jenkins might have been suspects, but Dalton Fowler was another case entirely. Dalton had been obsessed with Holly in high school and had followed her around everywhere she went, yet, as far as Tj knew, she never once gave him the time of day. Dalton still lived in Serenity and Tj knew him well. She couldn't imagine him as a killer but she could see how the original investigators might have honed in on him.

"There's a note at the bottom of the page," Tj commented. "It just says Rebecca H."

"Rebecca Heins. She did not attend the party and she was not considered at any point to be a suspect but she was a witness. Her witness statement is not public record because she was a minor and she came in voluntarily and asked not to be identified."

"Can you get her statement?"

"Maybe. I'll try."

"You know she works at Tiz the Season. I promised the girls I'd take them to get their Halloween costumes today. I think they wanted to go to that new costume shop in the strip mall outside of town but I think I can talk them into shopping locally. If Rebecca is working today, I'll see if she is willing to talk to me."

"Okay, if you discover anything relevant call me."

"I will. And I'll call you either way after I meet with the *Second Look* woman tomorrow. This should be interesting."

After Tj picked the girls up from The Antiquery, she headed toward Tiz the Season, a retail store specializing in seasonal inventory. The store was currently decked out with Halloween costumes and decorations, but Tj knew that once November first rolled around the Halloween items would be cleared out and Christmas gifts and decorations would take their place.

"Can I be a princess for Halloween?" Gracie asked.

"Haven't you been a princess the last two years?" Tj reminded her.

"Yes, but I really like being a princess. This year I want to be Cinderella."

"Being a princess is dumb," Ashley teased her sister. "I'm going to be a zombie. Or maybe a vampire."

"Zombies and vampires are scary," Gracie said. "I don't want to be scary. I want to be something pretty."

"You were Cinderella when you were a baby. You can't be Cinderella again," Ashley insisted.

"Can so."

"Cannot."

"You can be whatever you want," Tj told her youngest sibling. "And Ashley can be whatever she wants, as long as we can find costumes."

"I don't need a costume. I just need face paint," Ashley informed her. "Only babies wear packaged costumes."

"I'm not a baby," Gracie whined.

"Are so."

"Okay, that's enough arguing. The town is really beginning to look like a Halloween wonderland," Tj commented in an attempt to change the subject. The entire downtown section of the lakefront community was decorated for the upcoming Halloween festivities. Bright yellow aspen trees lining the sidewalks were draped with orange and white twinkle lights, while hundreds of scarecrows and huge orange pumpkins were displayed in front of brightly lit shops, inviting the casual passerby in from the crisp fall air. "The town really has pulled out all the stops. It will be fun to come down here on Halloween night and look at all the decorations. Maybe on our way back home from trick-or-treating."

"Aspen Maplewood is having a Halloween party this year," Ashley informed Tj. "Me and Kristi want to go to the party instead of trick-or-treating. Trick-or-treating is for toddlers."

"Is not," Gracie countered.

"Is so."

"I think a party sounds like fun," TJ interrupted the

argument. "I'll talk to Aspen's mom and work out the details."

"Please don't say anything to embarrass me when you talk to her," Ashley said.

"Why would you think I would embarrass you?"

"It's a coed party, so there'll be boys there. I can just picture you going on and on about how little Ashley is growing up and how the years simply fly by. Knowing you, you'll get all choked up and say something about how I'm becoming a woman right before your eyes."

"I wouldn't say that," Tj defended herself.

"You said that in pretty much those exact words when Jimmy's mom called to see if it was okay if I went to the movies with him."

"I guess I did do that," Tj admitted.

"It was the most embarrassing thing that has ever happened to me." Ashley groaned.

"I'm sorry. I promise I won't say anything embarrassing when I speak to Aspen's mom."

"Maybe Papa can talk to her. Or Aunt Jenna."

"I said I wouldn't embarrass you, and I won't."

Tj looked at Ashley in the rearview mirror. The look on her face indicated her life was over. Maybe she *was* becoming overly sentimental when it came to the girls. Ashley was right; she did tend to go on and on at times.

Pulling up in front of the seasonal store, Tj parked and turned off the engine. She reminded the girls to exit the vehicle on the sidewalk side.

"Let's start by looking for Gracie's Cinderella costume and then we can look for your spooky one after that," Tj suggested to Ashley.

"Aspen and a couple of my other friends are in the back of the store near the masks. I'll go hang out with them while you help Gracie."

"Okay, but don't leave the store and please stay out of trouble. I'll come find you in a few minutes."

Ashley called out to Aspen and then hurried away. When she'd first moved to Paradise Lake Ashley had been so angry over the death of her mother that she'd lashed out at everyone she came into contact with. The end result was that she'd had a difficult time making friends. Luckily, Jenna's eldest daughter Kristi, had not only befriended her but been patient with her mood swings. Eventually, Ashley had learned what it meant to be a friend and had developed a nice network of relationships.

"How come Ashley is nice to her friends but so mean to me?" Gracie asked.

"She's just getting to the age when she's trying to act cooler than she really is, so she compensates by making everyone crazy." Tj looked down at the adorable second grader beside her. "You aren't going to stop being my sweet little cupcake, are you?"

Gracie shook her head. "I'm never going to be mean like Ashley."

"Good." Tj took Gracie's hand in hers. "Let's go find you the best princess costume the store has left at a reasonable price."

Gracie skipped along beside her as she made her way to the princess aisle. As Gracie sorted through princess costumes, Tj looked around the store in the hope of spotting Rebecca. She supposed she could simply go up to the counter and ask if she was working today.

"Tj?" a woman Tj had gone to high school with said from behind her.

Tj turned around. "Vicki. How nice to see you. Are you in town for homecoming?"

She nodded. "I decided that as long as I was coming out west I'd get here a few days early to catch up with old friends. I'm here with Doreen Sullwold. She's buying a costume for her kindergartener."

Tj waved to Doreen, who was looking at a ladybug costume.

"Can you believe it's been ten years since we graduated?" Vicki asked.

"Actually, I can't. I work at the high school, but most days I still feel like a student."

"Is this your daughter?" Vicki nodded toward Gracie, who had just handed her sister the dress she'd been looking for.

"This is my sister Gracie. Half-sister, actually. Our mom died a couple of years ago, so Gracie and her sister Ashley came to live with me at the resort."

"So you never settled down with Hunter Hanson and had a family of your own?"

"No. Not yet, anyway."

Tj had dated Hunter all through high school. Everyone, including Tj, had thought they'd marry, but they'd ended up breaking up while they were in college. After they'd both returned to Serenity to pursue their careers there, they'd reestablished their friendship, but they hadn't started dating again until the previous winter.

"Will Hunter be at the reunion?"

"He will," Tj confirmed.

"It'll be nice to see him. Did he end up being a doctor like he always talked about?"

"Yes. His dad retired, so he's running the hospital."

"Good for him. It seems like our graduating class turned out all kinds of successful adults. I heard the reunion committee is expecting a good turnout."

"We are," Tj confirmed.

"I also heard there is a reporter in town asking a bunch of questions about the night Holly was murdered."

"That is true as well."

"It was such a horrible thing. I was questioned during the initial investigation. It was a terrifying experience. I was only seventeen at the time and the deputy who interviewed me was pretty terrifying, but luckily I had an alibi."

"You did?"

"Noreen and I arrived at the party together, left at the same time, and spent the night together. I'm pretty sure we were removed from the suspect list."

"I'm sure you were. And I'm really happy you are in town. It'll be fun to catch up. I really should get going," Tj said as she spotted Rebecca at the back of the store.

"Text me. We'll do lunch."

Tj looked down at Gracie. "Is this the dress you want?"

Gracie nodded. "I'll need shoes."

"I need to talk to a friend for a minute. I'm going to have you wait with Ashley for a few minutes and then we will look for your shoes."

"K."

Tj took Gracie's hand and headed toward the back of the store where Ashley was looking at masks.

"I changed my mind about the face paint," Ashley

informed Tj when she arrived with Gracie. "I want this instead."

Ashley held up a hideous mask.

"Looks like an easy costume. What are you going to wear with it?"

"I'm going to see if either Papa or Grandpa have an old shirt I can rip up. I'll just wear an old pair of jeans on the bottom."

"Wonderful. Sounds like the easiest costume ever. I need to talk to someone for a minute and I need you to watch Gracie."

Ashley snarled at her sister but didn't argue.

"I'll only be a minute I promise."

"Can we go look at the window display?" Gracie asked.

Tj glanced at Ashley. "Will you go with your sister and will you behave?"

Ashley shrugged. "Yeah. I wouldn't mind looking at the decorations."

Ashley took Gracie's hand and headed toward the front of the store while Tj headed toward the back of the store to find Rebecca.

"Just the woman I was looking for," Tj greeted Rebecca who was sorting through opened and discarded costumes.

"Hi Tj. Do you need help finding something?"

"Actually, if you have a few minutes, I wanted to talk to you about something other than costumes."

Rebecca handed Tj a witch's costume. "If you can talk while we fold I'm more than willing."

Tj folded the costume and added it to the stack before picking up another. "Have you heard that *Second Look* is coming to town to investigate Holly's murder?"

Rebecca frowned. "*Second Look* as in the television show?"

"That'd be the one."

"I hadn't heard. When is this happening?"

"Tomorrow actually. I was just over at the sheriff's office talking to Roy and he mentioned that you provided a witness statement back when the original investigation was going on."

Rebecca hesitated. "That was supposed to be anonymous."

"It was. I haven't seen the statement. Neither has Roy. He just knew that the deputies spoke to you at the time. I know you must have had your reasons for being anonymous at the time but I was hoping you might be willing to share what you know with me now."

"Why?"

"I'm being interviewed by the *Second Look* people tomorrow and I guess I just want to be as prepared as possible."

"Are you a suspect?"

"It seems I might be along with a handful of other people. I can assure you that I didn't kill Holly. I'd just like to help Roy. You know how shorthanded he is, and I have a feeling that things are about to get stirred up real fast."

"I voluntarily went into the sheriff's office ten years ago and gave an anonymous statement because I saw something no one knew that I saw. The deputies back then took my statement, but to be honest, it didn't seem like they followed up. I guess I don't know for certain that they didn't follow up but they never bothered to call me or ask me any further questions."

"Will you tell me what you saw?"

Rebecca hesitated. "Not here and not now. I'll call you."

"Okay, thanks. I'd appreciate that."

Tj texted Rebecca her number and then went to find her sisters. She supposed that Rebecca had a point. The middle of a crowded store wasn't the best place to share long buried secrets.

After the girls picked out their costumes and Tj paid for them they headed home. Tj felt a sense of contentment when she turned onto the resort road. It had been a productive afternoon and she'd managed to make a sizeable dent in her 'to do' list.

"Look at the lights," Gracie gasped.

"It looks like the staff finished the decorations." The staff had worked hard to make Maggie's Hideaway appear as a Halloween Village. Scarecrows and hay bales were displayed at the entrance and white lights had been hung in the aspen trees that lined the drive. The interior of the resort was likewise decorated for the upcoming holiday.

Tj and her family lived in a large private residence on the edge of the resort, providing them a degree of privacy while affording them the resources of the resort as a whole.

"Stop the car," Gracie screamed as Tj turned into the driveway to their home from the resort road.

Tj slammed on the brakes. "What's wrong?"

"I saw something."

"Like what?"

"A dog. I think it was a dog. It ran under that big bush when you turned the corner."

Tj looked around. She didn't see anything. "It's almost dark. It was probably a coyote."

"It wasn't a coyote. You have to go look."

She was willing to bet a week's pay Gracie had seen a coyote, or maybe even a raccoon. The chances that there was a stray dog this far from town were remote, but Tj knew Gracie wasn't going to let it go until she checked it out.

"You wait in the car in case it was a coyote," Tj said. Living at Paradise Lake, Tj was used to sharing her space with a lot of different wild animals, including bears and cougars, but the highest incidence of animal-to-people injuries seemed to come from the overly domesticated coyotes that roamed the area and weren't in the least afraid of people.

Tj pulled over to the side of the road, just in case another vehicle came in their direction. She took a flashlight from her glove box and opened the driver's side door, then slid out onto the narrow private road and made her way over to the large shrub Gracie had pointed to. If it was a coyote, it would most likely take off once she shone the light in its eyes. If it was a bear she was going to need to tread lightly. And if it was a cougar...well, Tj didn't want to think about that. Luckily, cougar sightings in populated areas were rare.

Tj shone the light into the dense shrub while she moved a thick branch to the side. "Well, I'll be."

Gracie had been right after all. Crouched down beneath the thick foliage was a golden retriever puppy.

"What are you doing all the way out here by yourself?"

The puppy whimpered.

"Don't worry. I'm not going to hurt you. I'll take you home and get you some dinner. Does that sound good?"

The pup hesitated.

"We have other animals. A dog, four cats, six horses, and a cow, to be specific."

The puppy just looked at her.

"The cow's name is Bruiser," Tj continued in a soft, soothing voice. "His arrival at the resort is really a funny story." Tj knelt down on the ground and tried to coax the puppy out. He was shaking in fear. The poor thing must have been through a pretty horrible ordeal to be this frightened. "If you come with me I can tell you all about it."

The pup scooted farther into the shrub. Tj was trying to decide what to do when suddenly the pup looked up and began wagging her tail.

"Come here, puppy."

Tj turned around. Gracie was out of the car and standing behind her. She wanted to scold her for disobeying, but the puppy ran right over to her.

"Can we keep her?" Gracie laughed as the puppy wagged her whole body while she licked her face.

"I think we need to make sure she isn't lost. We'll take her home and give her some dinner. Then I'll call Rosalie to come check her over." Rosalie Taylor was the town veterinarian and her dad's girlfriend. She was also the one responsible for Bruiser living at the resort. "We'll call the shelter and if no one claims her, then maybe we can talk to Papa about keeping her."

"I think Echo wants to have a puppy to play with," Gracie said persuasively. "We have four cats but only one dog."

"If we don't find the owner it will be up to Papa. I'm not sure Crissy is going to like having to share you with a puppy."

"She'll get used to her. Crissy got used to Echo, and she

didn't like him at all when she first came to live with us."

"That's true," Tj admitted.

"I'm going to name her Pumpkin because she's orange and it's Halloween," Gracie decided. "Can she sleep with me?"

"We'll see."

By the time the group walked in through the kitchen door dinner was on the table. Tj slipped a collar on the puppy and attached a leash. Then she gave her some food and water and tied her up close enough to the family so she wouldn't feel deserted in a strange environment, but far enough away so she wouldn't get the idea it was okay to lay under the table while the family was eating.

"Gracie made the finals for the spelling bee," Tj announced when everyone had been served.

"That's wonderful," Tj's father, Mike, or as the girls called him, Papa, exclaimed. "I knew all that practicing would pay off."

"I even beat Julie the brain." Gracie grinned. Julie often beat her in academic competitions. "She forgot the second S in misspell." Gracie giggled.

"Oh, that is funny." Tj laughed.

"She came in second, so she'll still get to go to the final round, but it was fun to win for once. Trisha was absent or she probably would have won, but I think she's going to be in the finals, too. My teacher said she was taking the top five spellers to the spell-off."

"You'll win," Ashley said with confidence. "Just don't overthink it. People tend to do that. Overthink things. The more you think about something you already know the more you might mess it up."

"Thanks, Ashley." Gracie smiled.

After Tj dinner was finished, Tj called Rosalie who came by and gave Pumpkin a clean bill of health. Mike and Rosalie settled in to watch a movie in the den while Tj got the girls to bed. Once everyone was settled she lit some pumpkin candles and curled up on the living room sofa in front of the fire. It had started to drizzle, and the long-range forecast called for rain for the next twenty-four hours at least. Tj's boyfriend Hunter Hanson had said he'd call when he got off work, but although it was almost eleven o'clock he'd yet to check in. She knew he must be dealing with some sort of an emergency and would call if he could. One of the difficult things about dating a doctor was the unpredictability of his hours.

Echo had curled up on the floor beneath her feet and Cuervo, her big orange tomcat, was curled up in her lap. Pumpkin had been thrilled to sleep on Gracie's bed and the other cats in residence had likewise found comfy places to settle in for the night.

The phone rang as Tj took a sip of her wine. It was Hunter.

"Hey, did you just get home?"

"Actually, I'm still at work," Hunter answered.

"I heard there was an accident on the summit."

"Yeah." Hunter sighed. "There was. It was a bad one. I'm exhausted, but I wanted to call to say good night. I should have tomorrow night off if you want to do something."

"That sounds fun as long as Samantha Colton doesn't dig up something that has me cowering in my room."

"Who's Samantha Colton and why would she have you cowering?"

Tj explained.

Hunter let out a long breath. "I'm not sure how well that's going to go over with our group, and it certainly will affect the weekend. Pretty much everyone who was at the party on the night Holly was murdered will be in town for the reunion."

"I suspect that's the reason Samantha Colton chose now to investigate this particular cold case," Tj said. "I'd love to find Holly's killer, but I agree that digging up the events surrounding the murder while everyone is in town is going to put a definite damper on the festivities. Still, I guess the woman is going to do what she's going to do. Maybe I can convince her to take a soft approach to the investigation. If Roy is right, her investigation is already responsible for Mia Monroe and Jada Jenkins bailing out."

"They aren't coming?"

Tj filled him in on what Colton had said to Mia. "And if that wasn't bad enough, she came right out and accused Jada of cheating on her midterm exams the first quarter of her senior year."

"What? Why would Jada cheat? She was the smartest student in the entire school next to Mackenzie Paulson."

"And you," Tj reminded Hunter. He had excelled academically, but he'd also played sports, which took up a lot of his time and prevented him from participating in some of the advanced classes that would have made him a contender for the coveted valedictorian spot.

"To be honest, when Roy first told me what Colton had accused Jada of doing, I outright insisted cheating wasn't even a possibility," Tj continued. "But then I remembered her mom and dad split up just as we began our senior year, and I seem to remember her missing a lot of school."

"That's right," Hunter said. "Now that you mention it, I remember that too."

"Yet she aced all her midterms."

"Maybe she got extra tutoring or studied at home even though she skipped classes," Hunter speculated.

"Maybe. But according to Roy, Colton accused Jada of cheating on her midterms in order to maintain her GPA, which she desperately needed to be accepted at MIT."

Hunter didn't say anything, but Tj was sure he was frowning. "Did Jada tell Roy that?"

"No, Colton did. She told Roy she believes Holly somehow found out Jada cheated and threatened to tell the administration unless she used her tech know-how to break into the email accounts of some of our fellow students."

"The whole thing sounds fishy to me," Hunter declared. "First of all, how did Holly find out Jada cheated, if she really did? And second, why did Holly want access to the student accounts?"

"Roy said Colton didn't know the answer to either of these questions but intended to find out."

"Okay, then maybe a better question is, how did Colton find all of this out?" Hunter asked.

"Someone must be talking."

"Yeah, but who would know any of this except Jada and Holly? Holly is dead and Jada would have no reason to bring it up herself."

Tj thought about it. "The only person who comes to mind is Jessie Baldwin. Jessie and Holly were best friends. It stands to reason that if Holly did have this information, she would have shared it with Jessie. The thing I can't figure out is why Jessie would share the information with Colton. And when would she have shared it? According to Roy, Colton was in LA yesterday, and he said I'm her first appointment in Serenity, so when could she have spoken to Jessie, or anyone else for that matter?"

Cuervo tried to knock the phone out of Tj's hand. Apparently, he'd decided she'd ignored him long enough. Tj adjusted her position so the cat could climb into her lap while she waited for Hunter to respond.

"As you said, Holly was Jessie's best friend," Hunter said. "If I were Colton I'd start with the best friend. She probably already interviewed her, maybe over the phone, and I'm betting Jessie shared what she knows. I'm sure she'd want Holly's killer found, no matter who it might be."

"I guess that makes sense. I don't want our reunion ruined, but I am sort of curious to find out what else Colton might have dug up. I've seen *Second Look* a couple of times. In most cases the investigators dig up as much evidence as they can before they show up on location. The show actually has a pretty good success rate. I'm betting Holly's killer will be pretty nervous when they find out who Samantha Colton is and what she's doing in town."

CHAPTER 3

Tuesday, October 27

As far as Tuesdays went, this one was shaping up to be one of the oddest she'd had in a while. She woke up to a torrential downpour that caused the small creek that ran behind the house to overflow, flooding the basement. By the time she'd helped her dad and grandpa redirect the water and mop up the mess, she'd barely had time to grab a cup of coffee before she had to hop into the shower to get ready for work. As she hurriedly rushed from her bathroom into her bedroom to dress for the day ahead, she tripped over Pumpkin, who had wandered in through the partially open door. The bruise on her arm was painful but not dire, but the one on her cheek was going to cause her more anguish than she was prepared to deal with.

After ushering her sisters through the steady rain and into the 4Runner she turned the ignition switch only to find the battery was completely dead. Luckily, her dad was still at the house, so she enlisted his help to drive her and the girls into town. After saying her goodbyes to her sisters at the front entry, where the hallway to the elementary school veered to the left and the hallway to the high school veered to the right, she headed toward the teachers' lounge on the high school side of the building. Even with all the delays, she'd made it to work with a few minutes to spare.

"Coach Jensen." Carly poked her head in the door of Tj's office just as she'd sat down at her desk. "You wanted to see me again?"

"Yes. Come in and take a seat."

"Did someone hit you?" Carly frowned as she sat down across from Tj.

"I tripped over the puppy my sister found last night and hit my face on the dresser."

Carly raised one eyebrow in an expression of doubt.

"I know that sounds like a cover-up—the type of story someone who *had* been hit in the face would tell—but it really is what happened," Tj assured her.

"Maybe some makeup?"

"Makeup might be a good idea," Tj acknowledged. She had a feeling this was going to be a *very* long day. "I asked you to stop by because—"

"You've changed your mind about the suspension?" Carly interrupted hopefully.

"No, I'm afraid I really can't do that. But I do have a proposal for you."

"A proposal?"

"I've spoken to Principal Remington and he's agreed to reevaluate the length of your suspension if you're willing to make some concessions."

Carly frowned but didn't say anything.

"Basically, as things stand now, your suspension runs until the end of the soccer season. We still have four weeks in the regular season and then the play-offs. Principal Remington is willing to reevaluate after two weeks if you'll apologize to both the girl you elbowed and her coach and agree to counseling. You'll also need to work as a nonparticipating member of the team during those two weeks."

Tj could see Carly was about to refuse.

"Principal Remington is being more than fair. I'd take him up on his offer if you care about your chances for a scholarship."

"What kind of counseling?"

"Mrs. Remington will arrange for you to see a psychologist she knows who specializes in both grief counseling and anger management. Dr. Cowell will meet with you here on campus at no cost to you or your mother."

Carly bit her lip as she considered the proposal.

"I spoke with him after my mom died," Tj said. "He's good at what he does. He's a kind and caring man. I think you'll like him."

"He helped you?"

Tj nodded. "He worked with my sister Ashley as well. Like you, she tended to work out her anger and grief with her fists. She still lashes out at times, but I think Dr. Cowell really helped her to learn impulse control."

Carly appeared to consider her options. She squirmed around in her chair in a way that indicated she'd rather be anywhere else, but she didn't bolt as Tj had half-expected she would.

"And the work thing?" Carly asked.

"You'd be my assistant and do whatever I ask you to do. Additionally, you'd attend all practices and games, but you wouldn't be allowed to suit up until after the suspension is lifted."

Carly smiled. "I can be your assistant?"

"In a menial labor sort of way."

"Okay. I agree to Remington's terms. But how am I supposed to apologize to the girl I elbowed? The team was visiting from Reno."

"I'll arrange for you to make the apology via Skype. I'll let you know the details once I work them out. We have practice at our regular time this afternoon, so I expect you to head over to my office as soon as your fifth-period class is over."

"Okay. I'll be here."

"And Carly...when you meet with Dr. Cowell, give him a chance. I know you don't think counseling will help, and I can't guarantee anything, but it might."

"Does my mother know about it?"

"Principal Remington spoke to her this morning. She indicated she wouldn't force you to see the man if you didn't want to, but she wouldn't interfere if you were willing."

"In other words she doesn't care one way or the other, just like she no longer seems to care about anything."

"I think she cares," Tj reassured her. "But we both know this whole thing has been hard on her. Maybe if you're able to work through things you can help your mom to work through her grief as well."

Carly didn't answer. She simply stood up and thanked Tj for finding a solution that would let her stay with the team. Tj let out the breath she'd been holding after Carly left her office. Hopefully, Carly would take this chance she'd been given and make the most of it. She'd had a rough couple of months. There was nothing anyone could do about Kenny's death. All Tj could do was help Carly move past it to the best of her ability.

Later that afternoon Tj sat with Gina during lunch. "Teens these days have it tough," Tj said between bites of her tuna sandwich. "Not only do they have to deal with bullying on campus, but they also have to worry about someone posting embarrassing photos of them to all their friends with the click of a cell phone camera."

"I take it you talked to Lexi?" Gina asked.

"I tried," Tj answered as she opened a bag of potato chips. "I called her, but she said she didn't want to talk about it. She's totally mortified. She swears she's never coming back to school. I wish I could figure out a way to help her. Even if we catch the person responsible, it won't erase the embarrassment she's feeling."

"Lexi's little song and dance in the shower *was* embarrassing," Gina admitted, "but with the exception of some side boob the wall hid her private parts. I would be just as mortified if it had happened to me, but Lexi can't allow this bully to ruin her life. There has to be something we can do to change her mind. Did you speak to her mother?"

"No, but Principal Remington did. She wants to give Lexi time. She told him Lexi threatened to run away if she tried to force her to go to school. I might try to talk to Lexi's mom myself if I get the opportunity. She went to this school, you know."

"She did?"

"Yeah. She was far enough ahead of me that we weren't here at the same time, but I know who she is. The really sad thing is that when she was in school *she* was the bully."

A look of surprise and disbelief crossed Gina's face. "Get out."

"It's true." Tj took a sip of her soda before she continued. "She was the queen bee of Serenity High School her entire four years. Chantel was head cheerleader, homecoming queen, and undeniable *it* girl during her reign. From what I've been told by my friends who have older brothers and sisters, she either liked you or she didn't, and if she didn't, she treated you like dirt."

"But Lexi is so sweet," Gina countered. "I can't believe she was raised by a queen bee."

"Believe it. Like I said, I didn't know Chantel well, but I knew who she was. Her reputation was widespread in the community as a whole, not just in the high school. She was really stunning. Everyone thought she would grow up to be a famous actress or a supermodel."

"So why didn't she?" Gina asked as she finished the salad she'd brought from home.

"She got pregnant and became a single mom when she was just eighteen."

"Oh, wow. Was the father in the picture?"

"No. To be honest, I don't know who the father even was. I've looked at Lexi's student records and there isn't a father listed. Lexi's emergency contact is a family friend."

"It's hard to grow up without a dad," Gina commented as she began gathering her trash.

"I have a great one," Tj said, "but I grew up without a mom, and it *is* hard. In any case, I imagine having to raise a baby on her own humbled Chantel. I still don't know her well, but I've seen her around town and we've worked together on a few committees. We've never really talked on any sort of personal level, but it seems she's managed to put her bullying aside and has turned out to be a really nice lady who cares deeply about her daughter."

"So the bully's daughter became the victim. That would be almost poetic if it wasn't so sad. Lexi is a great kid. We need to find a way to help her."

CHAPTER 4

Samantha Colton was an absolutely stunning woman. She was at least six feet tall, making Tj, who stood at five foot nothing, feel like a child. Her dark hair was pulled back to show off her flawless mocha skin and deep, dark eyes.

"Ms. Jensen."

"Tj is fine. May I call you Samantha?"

"If you wish."

"Please have a seat," Tj offered.

Samantha sat down and crossed her legs. She took a pen and a small notebook out of the large bag she carried. "I know you only have fifty minutes until your next class, so I'll be brief."

"Okay."

"I have a list of students who attended the party the night Holly Riverton was murdered that I obtained from the sheriff's report. I'd like you to look at it to see if it's accurate to the best of your knowledge and memory."

Tj looked at the paper. There were initially just ten students. Jenna, Dennis, Hunter, and Tj had arrived just after Brett, his date Jessie, and Jessie's best friend Holly.

Shortly after they got there, Nathan Fullerton and Jada Jenkins had shown up. Within thirty minutes after that Mia Monroe had arrived alone.

During the evening at least ten other students had come and gone, including Mackenzie Paulson, who ended up being the class valedictorian, and several members of the football team who arrived with the female groupies who tended to follow them around.

Tj also remembered seeing Vicki Davis, Doreen Sullwold, Dalton Fowler and Teddy Bolton. As far as Tj could tell, the list was accurate, but there could have been others who'd stopped by for a short visit before moving on.

"To the best of my knowledge the list is correct."

"Can you walk me through the events of that evening?" Colton asked.

"A bunch of us were hanging out in the parking lot in front of the school after the homecoming dance when Brett pulled up in his new Mustang and invited everyone who was standing there to a party at his house."

"Was that normal behavior?" Samantha wondered.

Tj frowned.

"Did Brett Conrad often throw parties to which he invited friends from a wide array of social groups?"

"No. Actually, Brett was known for throwing parties that specifically excluded anyone who wasn't a member of the popular crowd."

"So his behavior that evening was atypical?"

"Yes, I guess it was."

She jotted down some notes.

"Had you been to parties at Brett Conrad's house prior to that night?"

"Plenty of times," Tj answered. "Brett was the captain of the football team and I was a cheerleader. We hung out with the same kids most of the time."

"Once you arrived did you notice anything was different from other parties you'd attended at Brett's house?"

Tj thought about it. There had been an odd vibe that night, but she couldn't put her finger on the reason. "It seemed like everyone was really amped up," Tj answered honestly. "I don't know it for certain, but if I had to guess I'd say the punch was spiked with something other than light rum."

"And did Brett Conrad supply the punch?"

"I believe so. It was there when we arrived."

"Did Brett normally serve rum punch at his parties?"

Tj furrowed her brow. "No. In fact, he always served beer. I remember thinking it was odd he served that fruity punch. It really wasn't his style at all."

"Do you think Brett could have spiked the punch with something stronger than rum to create a distraction?"

"You think Brett killed Holly?"

"Do you?"

"Absolutely not. I'll admit the party was different than usual, but Holly was Jessie's best friend. Jessie was devastated when she died. Brett loved Jessie. He'd never do that to her, even if he did think Holly was a pest."

Colton stopped writing and looked directly at Tj. "Brett thought Holly was a pest?"

Tj hesitated. "He mentioned to me a time or two that Jessie seemed to do whatever Holly told her to do, and that it caused friction in their relationship, but he wouldn't kill Holly over something like that."

"According to my notes, Brett went on to marry Jessie Baldwin. Do you know if Holly would have approved of such a union had she lived?"

Tj was pretty sure Holly had all but convinced Jessie to break up with Brett before she died. Surely Brett hadn't done what it suddenly appeared he had a motive to do.

"I'm not really sure," Tj answered. "Holly and Brett didn't really get along, but I doubt she would have interfered in their relationship if she thought Jessie's feelings for Brett were real."

"Were they?"

Tj just looked at Colton.

"Jessie's feelings for Brett. Were they real?"

"She married him," Tj pointed out.

Colton tilted her head. She looked as if she were considering the situation.

"Are Brett and Jessie still married?"

"They are."

"Do they have children?"

"No, they don't."

"Have you spent any time with them as a couple since graduation?" she asked.

"No," Tj admitted.

"And yet you were close in high school?"

Tj shrugged. "We were friends. Good friends. But it isn't odd that we didn't stay in touch. A lot of the kids I grew up with moved on to other things after college. Serenity is a small town. It isn't odd for young adults to move on."

Colton jotted down a few more notes. The woman was a skillful interviewer. Tj was certain that she was trying to trip her up and make her say something she didn't mean to say.

"Is it true that Jessie considered breaking things off with Brett prior to Holly's death?"

"I don't know. I guess you'll have to ask her about her thoughts at the time."

"Can you confirm that Jessie entered into a flirtation with Nathan Fullerton shortly before the homecoming dance?"

Tj gave Colton a sharp look. "How do you know that?"

She shrugged. "I have my sources."

No one other than Jessie, Holly, Nathan, and Tj knew about that spontaneous make-out session after cheer practice the day before homecoming. Holly was dead, Tj sure hadn't told anyone, and she doubted Jessie would admit to it, which left Nathan as the source by default.

"So it's true?" Colton prompted.

"Yes. Sort of. Nathan stopped by practice the day before the game to ask the cheer coach a few questions for an article he was writing about homecoming for the paper. She was busy, so he stayed to watch. Jessie and Nathan kept eyeing each other, but I didn't think she would risk what she had with Brett to date Nathan, who is famous now but was pretty much a nerd back then. After everyone had left I realized I'd left my pompoms on the bleachers and went back to get them. That's when I saw Jessie and Nathan together."

"Who else might have seen them?" she asked.

"Holly was there, but I didn't see anyone else around."

"Did you think it odd that Holly was watching her best friend make out rather than leaving and offering them privacy?"

"Yeah, I thought it was strange, but Holly and Jessie had an unusual relationship."

"Unusual how?" Colton asked.

Tj paused. "They were really close, which I guess isn't unusual. My best friend and I were closer than sisters in high school and we still are. It just seemed Jessie and Holly had a more possessive relationship."

"Possessive?"

Tj bit her lip. "It's hard to explain. Sometimes they seemed like more than friends. Almost like..."

"Lovers?"

Tj frowned. "Maybe. I mean, it never occurred to me back then, but now that I think about it." Tj scrunched up her nose. "But that can't be right. Jessie is married to Brett. She can't be gay."

"Being gay and having a marriage with someone of the opposite sex aren't mutually exclusive," Colton said. "And I'm not suggesting Jessie is gay. I'm simply suggesting she may have shared an intense relationship with a specific person during her teen years."

"So what are you saying? Now you think Jessie might've killed Holly?"

"I'm not saying anything," she said. "I'm just asking questions.

Tj squirmed in her chair. She suddenly felt as though she was on trial. Samantha Colton had a presence that couldn't be ignored.

Before this conversation Tj had been certain none of her friends could be responsible for Holly's death, but now she realized she was suspicious of all of them. The woman certainly knew how to dig up whatever dirt there was to be found. Tj just hoped she wasn't next. Not that she had anything to hide. Or at least she didn't think she did.

"I understand Holly had a suitor herself before her death," Colton stated.

"I'm not sure I'd call him a suitor, but yeah, there was a guy who had a huge crush on her. He sent her notes and followed her around. He's a nice guy now, but he was a real pest back then."

"And the name of this pest?"

"Dalton Fowler."

"And was Dalton a member of Holly's social group?"

"No," Tj said. "Holly was firmly established as a member of the elite group, which was mainly made up of jocks and cheerleaders, while Dalton was a nerd. He never had a chance with her, but that didn't keep him from trying."

"Does Dalton Fowler still live in Serenity?" she asked.

"He does, and like I said, he's a really nice guy now. He's a respected contractor, husband, and father. We serve on the PTA together for the elementary school. He's a totally different person than he was in high school, and no, I don't think he killed Holly."

"And why is that?" Colton asked.

"Why is what?"

"You said you didn't think Dalton killed Holly. Why?"

"He was totally in love with her."

"It sounds like he was obsessed with her," she said.

Tj hesitated. The last thing she wanted to do was get Dalton or anyone else in trouble. "I suppose *obsessed* would be an accurate word. But, like I said, he's different now. He's grown up."

Colton shifted her position in her chair. She flipped her notepad to a new page and jotted down a few items.

"We're trying to establish whether eighteen-year-old

Dalton Fowler could have killed Holly Riverton. The person he has become is irrelevant."

Tj supposed she had a point.

"According to the initial sheriff's report, Dalton Fowler was at the party."

"Yes, he was," Tj confirmed.

"Did he bring a date?"

"No. He came alone."

"Did Holly have a date?" she asked.

"No. At least not for the party. She had a date to the dance but he didn't come to the party with her."

"And this date's name?"

"Dusty Baker."

"Would you say that Dusty and Holly were dating at the time?"

Tj frowned. "No not at all. I really don't know why they went to the dance together."

"Does Mr. Baker still live in town?"

"No. I haven't seen him since high school."

Colton jotted down a few more notes. "I understand there was at least one member of the high school staff at the party."

"One of the teachers stopped by for a few minutes to congratulate Brett and the team members who were at his house. He didn't stay long."

"And this staff member's name?"

Tj hesitated. In spite of the fact that Jim Hanover had turned into a stick in the mud she no longer got along with, she didn't want to get him into trouble.

Still, based on Colton's comments, Tj was willing to bet she already knew.

"His name is Jim Hanover."

"And he's still on staff at this institution?"

Tj nodded.

"Would you say it was normal behavior for Mr. Hanover to attend student parties?"

Tj took a deep breath. "Not currently, but he was a new teacher ten years ago and, like many new and young teachers, he developed close relationships with his students. He didn't really attend the party. Like I said, he just stopped by to congratulate the guys. I doubt he was there more than thirty minutes."

Colton frowned but didn't say anything. Then she continued. "What can you tell me about Mia Monroe?"

Tj chose her words carefully. "You know how every high school has that one student with enough self-esteem to *actually* not care what others think of her? That was Mia. She knew who she was and she wasn't afraid to march to the beat of her own drum. At our school, Mia was the girl we all wished we could be."

"Can you expand on that?" she asked.

"Most teens want to be accepted. They each have their own way of accomplishing that, but Mia just didn't seem to care what others thought. She was the only student at Serenity High School who really seemed free of all the social constraints of fitting in. She was a unique individual."

"I agree."

Tj frowned. Roy told her Colton had accused Mia of having the personality of a killer.

"I see by your expression that you already spoke to Deputy Fisher. I realize I was hard on Ms. Monroe at first, but I had to be certain. I've come to the conclusion that she is what she appears to be: an independent soul with a free spirit."

"Maybe you should tell her that," Tj scolded. "Do you know she decided not to come to the reunion after your interview with her?"

"If she's the person we both think she is, she didn't cancel because of something I said. If I were you, I would look more closely at her real motive."

Tj frowned. What real motive? Tj suspected Colton had a lot more information than she was sharing.

"So let's talk about the rivalry for homecoming queen between you and Holly."

Darn. Tj hoped she'd skip right over that. "What about it?"

"You were both vying for the same position?"

"Along with three other girls."

"Were these three other girls at the party?"

"No," Tj admitted. "Let me save you some time with the questions. I'm not saying this to brag but I was popular in high school. Very popular. Everyone knew I was going to be homecoming queen long before the students even voted. Holly was also popular but she tended to exist more on the fringe of the student body. When she decided to run for homecoming queen everyone was surprised, when she won everyone was astonished. I was convinced she cheated. She just wasn't that popular and not a single person I spoke to admitted to voting for her. I will admit that I was somewhat shallow in high school and being queen was important to me so I tried in an unsuccessful bid to have the votes recounted. Yes I was mad, and yes I said some things to some of my friends that might be construed as threatening, but I promise you I did not kill Holly. I was with my boyfriend Hunter for most of the evening on the night she died. You can ask him."

"I plan to." Samantha closed her notebook just as a bell rang in the distance. "We're out of time. I'll be in touch."

With that she was gone.

CHAPTER 5

Thankfully, Tj's dad had gotten her 4Runner running and had left it for her in the school parking lot so that she would be able to drop her sisters off at dance that afternoon. After that she headed toward the modest house where Chantel and Lexi Michaels lived. The house was small, but the yard was well kept and the porch was seasonally decorated, giving the property a welcoming feel. Lexi opened the door several seconds after Tj knocked.

"Coach Jensen. What are you doing here?"

"I'm here to speak to your mom, actually. I called ahead; she's expecting me."

Lexi opened the door to allow Tj to come inside. "I'm not going back to school. Ever."

"Yes, I've heard that's your stance. We really missed you at soccer practice today. You know the left side totally falls apart when you aren't there."

Lexi frowned but didn't say anything.

"Coach Jensen," Chantel greeted as she glided into the room. "I thought we'd chat on the back patio if that's okay with you."

"Patio? It's pouring rain."

"It's an enclosed patio."

"Oh, then that would be great." Tj smiled at Lexi and then followed Chantel down the hall to the back of the house.

The patio, like the rest of the home, was compact but well-tended. Tj took a seat at the glass table positioned on the center of the brick entertainment area, which was covered and completely walled in with glass.

"Thank you for meeting with me," Tj said.

Chantel really was beautiful. Her dark hair, blue eyes, flawless skin, and perfect smile topped a figure that even fashion models would envy. The current *it* girls at Serenity High seemed plastic in appearance, which paled in comparison to Chantel's effortless, natural look.

"I guess you know I'm concerned about Lexi," Tj began. "She's such a great kid. One of my favorite students, in fact. She's kind and hardworking, and she has a bright future ahead of her. I hate to see it ruined by some bully."

Chantel gave a sad little smile. "I agree with you. I've thought about the situation a lot since I found out what happened. I'll admit to being at a loss as to how to proceed. I want what's best for Lexi but I just don't see how I can ask her to go back to that school. Kids can be so cruel."

"They really can."

"It's funny. Not ha-ha funny but ironic. Lexi comes from a long line of women who bullied other people, and now she's the one being bullied."

Tj exhibited a look of surprise that Chantel would speak so openly.

"It's true. My grandmother was a bully, and she brought my mother up to be one too. My mother was absolutely stunning. The world stood in line to do her bidding and she knew it. By the time I was in the fourth grade, she'd passed on all her secrets to me. I knew how to demand respect and to own any environment in which I found myself. I cringe now when I look back at the way I treated others. Popularity isn't something you're handed; it's something you earn every day of your life. You have to know how to work it, and then you have to fight to stay on top."

"But why would anyone want to go through all that?" Tj asked.

Chantel shrugged. "It becomes a way of life. Once you've tasted the power that comes with living in the number-one spot, you realize you'll never settle for less. You'll do whatever it takes to maintain your position."

"Even knocking others down in the process?"

"Even that," Chantel admitted.

"Why hasn't Lexi followed in the tradition of the other women in your family? She's stunning. She's bright and athletic and could easily be Serenity High's *it* girl, but she's managed to stay grounded."

Chantel took a deep breath. "I got pregnant with Lexi when I was just seventeen. The boy I'd been dating dumped me when he found out I was going to have a baby, so I became a single mom at eighteen. My own mother was mortified and disowned me. I vowed not only to turn over a new leaf but to make sure the cycle was broken and Lexi didn't grow up with unrealistic social expectations. It seems, however, that all I've managed to accomplish is to turn her into a victim."

"Do you have any idea who would do this to her?" Tj asked.

Chantel frowned. "I'm not sure. I'd definitely look at the

girls at the top of the social hierarchy. The girls who have the most to lose. Being number one is exhausting. It's like juggling cats. You don't dare stop for fear the other girls will scratch your eyes out. The level of stress that comes with the position can make you do horrible things. I'd also look at anyone on the way up. Someone who wants to gain acceptance from the most popular girls. There are social climbers who will do anything to earn a place in the spotlight."

"Anyone else?" Tj asked.

"The girls at the bottom of the social hierarchy who might be jealous that Lexi is naturally smart and beautiful. The girls who would knock her down to feel better about themselves."

"You've basically just described every girl at Serenity High," Tj pointed out.

Chantel laughed. "Yes, I guess I have."

"So we've now identified the fact that virtually anyone has the potential to be a bully. How do we stop this from happening again and again?"

Chantel appeared to be thinking about it. "I guess if you can't stop the bullying, you stop the effect of the bullying."

Tj frowned.

"People who bully do so to get a reaction. They want the targeted person to be mortified. They want to put them in their place, so to speak; by doing so, they earn prestige. They feed on the fear. They feed on causing anguish to another person. The true byproduct of bullying comes from the person being bullied, not the person doing the bullying." At Tj's confused expression, Chantel leaned forward and looked her in the eye. "What if I filmed you doing something embarrassing and then uploaded it to all of my social networks with the intention of causing you distress? Maybe, like Lexi, you were singing in the shower."

Tj cringed at the thought.

"But what if when you saw the video you laughed and shrugged it off? What if you responded to the video by jumping around the room with your hands in the air in a victory dance, yelling, 'Dig me. Aren't I awesome? I bet none of you can pull off that tune the way I can.' Everyone would laugh *with* you rather than *at* you, and the bully would have been robbed of her power."

A light went on for Tj. "Oh, I get it. In order to be a bully, the person doing the bullying needs to get a reaction out of the intended victim."

"Exactly."

"I have an idea," Tj said. "Will you help me?"

"If it will help Lexi, I'm in."

After Tj left Chantel and Lexi's, she headed to the dance studio to pick up her sisters as well as Jenna's daughters, Kristi and Kari. She'd arranged to meet Jenna at the Antiquery prior to their evening out. After checking the movie lineup, they'd determined the first movie to be shown that night was family friendly, so they'd agreed to let Ashley and Kristi see it alone while they took the two younger girls into town to look at the decorations.

"They're running a few minutes late," one of the moms informed Tj when she hurried in through the front door of the studio. She shook out her umbrella and then hung it on one of the pegs provided for that purpose.

"Did Miss Marcia say anything about the costumes for the Christmas recital?" Tj asked as she peeled off her wet coat.

"Only that each student would need to bring in ninety dollars by November first. She's going to order them for everyone from the same supplier she used for the spring recital."

Between Halloween and dance recitals, Tj figured she'd need to get a second job to pay for costumes. Not that it wasn't worth it. Watching her sisters excel at something they loved was totally worth the effort and expense required. Last spring the group had performed a dance version of *The Wizard of Oz* and Gracie had been the Cowardly Lion. She'd been adorable. Tj had a photo of Gracie alongside Ashley, who had been a flying monkey, hanging on the wall in her bedroom.

"Did Miss Marcia mention the theme?" Tj asked.

"She's planning to do *The Nutcracker* again. Personally, I think she should mix it up. This is the third time in the past five years she's done the same ballet."

"A lot of the parents enjoy that ballet, and it's fun to see your child progress to bigger parts as she gets older," another mother joined in.

Tj was about to chime in when the front door opened, allowing rain and cold air to blow into the warm room.

"Oh, good, I'm not late." Marianne Fowler hurried in through the front door. "Some woman from TV came by to talk to Dalton at the site he was working at this afternoon. I'm not sure what she wanted, but he seemed really upset when he got home from work. I tried to get him to talk about it, but he wasn't sharing, then I realized I'd be late picking up the girls. I kept picturing them waiting out in the rain during my entire drive over here."

Tj found it hard to look Marianne in the eye after she'd basically turned the she-wolf on to Dalton's scent. She hadn't meant to offer Dalton up as a possible suspect in Holly's murder, but Samantha Colton had a way of getting information out of you whether you wanted to provide it or not.

"Miss Marcia is running late," one of the other moms responded. "It's a good thing too, because it really is coming down. I bet we're going to have major flooding by tomorrow. There's even talk the schools might close."

"What TV woman?" another mom asked. "Is Dalton going to be on TV?"

"I'm not sure," Marianne answered. "He really didn't want to talk about it."

"I bet he's going to get some sort of service award for all the labor he's donated to rebuild the part of the library that was damaged in the last storm," one of the moms said. "I just hope we don't have a repeat of the damage from this storm."

"But why would he be upset about getting an award?" Marianne asked.

"I guess that's true. Maybe someone is in town to report about the storm and they interviewed Dalton on account of him being a lifelong resident."

"Again, why would he be upset by that? Besides, it sounds like this woman sought him out specifically. Talking about the storm seems like more of a man-on-the-street feature."

"Maybe someone found his long-lost father and wants to reunite them on television," someone suggested.

"Dalton's father lives in Baltimore. We just visited him last summer," Marianne said. "His gout was acting up and he was in a lot of pain, so it wasn't a very pleasant visit. I never met anyone who can complain the way that man can."

"Maybe Dalton won the lottery," another bored mom suggested. "A big one, where they notify you in person."

"They don't notify you in person, no matter how much you win," someone else said.

Tj rolled her eyes. This was exactly how rumors got started. Someone would speculate about what was going on and then someone else would report that speculation as fact. Poor Dalton was in for a week filled with well-wishers congratulating him on winning the lottery, receiving an award, and finding his long-lost father. Still, Tj supposed it was better than everyone knowing the truth, so she kept her mouth shut. Only a few more minutes and she could collect the girls and head to the Antiquery.

CHAPTER 6

The Antiquery was both a café that served breakfast and lunch and an antique store that sold treasures collected by Jenna's mother Helen. One of the things Tj liked the most about visiting the Antiquery was that it always smelled amazing. Today the scent of cinnamon and pumpkin lingered in the air.

"Perfect timing," Jenna said as Tj walked in through the back door. "I'm just finishing up."

"What smells so wonderful in here?" Tj asked.

"I was baking the cookies the senior center ordered for their bingo night tonight."

"Do I smell pumpkin?" Tj asked.

"I have both pumpkin snickerdoodles and apple delight," Jenna confirmed. "Would you like to try one?"

"I would."

"Girls?" Jenna asked Ashley, Gracie, Kristi, and Kari. All four girls held out their hands for a cookie.

"I'll box them up and then we'll need to get going. I hoped Mom would be here to deliver the cookies, but she got tied up at the auction she attended today, so we'll need to drop them off on our way."

"We don't have time to stop at the senior center," Ashley complained. "We need to hurry if we're going to stop for dinner before we go to the movie."

"I'll hurry at the senior center, and I thought we'd stop to pick up some tacos," Jenna said. "They're having a special and they're fast, so we should have plenty of time to eat and get you to the movie on time."

"Can we get ice cream?" Kari asked.

"Once we drop off the older girls we can do whatever you and Gracie want," Jenna promised. "Kristi, can you run around to the loading door and make sure it's locked?"

Ashley followed Kristi as she trotted off toward the antique side of the store. When they'd converted the space, they'd added a large garage-style door off the alley to use for loading and unloading the antique furniture Helen purchased to refinish and sell. What had started as a hobby had turned into a lucrative career, and Helen had a good eye for which pieces would bring a big profit. In Tj's opinion, it was the way she artfully displayed the finished pieces in period arrangements that set her antique business above the rest.

"I noticed you finished redecorating your front window," Tj said as Jenna packaged the baked goods she'd prepared. "It looks really good. Spooky yet friendly."

"Thanks. I spent most of the morning working on it. I wanted to do something special since most of our graduating class will be in town to see it. I'm sure it doesn't compare to the big city windows many of our former classmates are used to, but I think it turned out nice."

"I love it. I'm really in the Halloween spirit despite being so busy this week."

"Things crazy at work?"

"They are, and in addition to Halloween, we have the reunion, homecoming, and tons of people in town."

"I imagine the resort is booked for the weekend thanks to the reunion," Jenna speculated.

"We've been booked for this weekend for at least two months. Still, with *Second Look* investigating Holly's death, I wouldn't be surprised if we have some cancelations."

Jenna set the boxes she'd finished filling to the side. "Did you meet with Samantha Colton today?"

"I did."

"And?"

"I'll tell you about it later, when there aren't little ears to overhear."

"I don't have little ears," Gracie complained. "They're the right size for my body."

Tj laughed. "That's not what I meant."

"I guess I'm ready," Jenna said. "But it appears we lost Kristi and Ashley."

"I'll load the younger two into your car while you fetch the older ones," Tj offered.

"There's an extra booster seat in the cargo area if you want to use it for Gracie rather than moving the one from your car into mine. Oh, and grab those two boxes. I'm going to donate some day-old pastries to the senior center as long as I have to stop there anyway."

They dropped off the cookies, grabbed a quick meal, and left the two older girls at the movie theater. Gracie and Kari decided they wanted to go to the video arcade at Rob's Pizza rather than walk around town because it was still raining. That gave Tj and Jenna the opportunity to catch up, sharing adult conversation over a glass of wine on the sidelines.

"So tell me about your meeting with Samantha Colton," Jenna said. "I've been even more anxious to hear after your cryptic comment."

"She's really good at what she does. In just thirty minutes, she had me half-believing practically everyone at the party that night could have killed Holly."

"What?" Jenna frowned. "Why would any of us kill Holly?"

Tj filled her friend in on the interview that afternoon while Jenna sipped her wine and listened intently. Based on the changing emotions mirrored on Jenna's face, she was as shocked by Samantha's suggestions as Tj had been. The thought that someone at the party could actually be a killer was disconcerting.

Tj had known most of the partygoers since they were all in kindergarten together. She couldn't imagine any of them doing such a horrendous thing, but one thing was certain: someone had.

"I guess it *was* sort of odd that Brett invited over everyone who just happened to be standing around in the parking lot, and I never really stopped to wonder about the punch," Jenna admitted. "And I do remember that Brett really didn't care for Holly, but I don't think he'd kill her. And the stuff about Jessie and Holly being lovers is ridiculous."

"Is it?"

"Surely you aren't buying that theory."

Tj shrugged. "At first I thought it was nuts, and maybe it is, but there was something different about their relationship. You and I were practically sisters, then and now, but we each have our own lives. Holly and Jessie definitely seemed to share a connection that was more intimate. I'm not saying they were lovers. In fact, I'd be surprised if that suggestion turns out to have any merit. But Samantha Colton's comment did get me thinking about what things were like. Don't you remember how Jessie was always making decisions based on Holly's opinion? High school girls do tend to lean on their best friends and the opinions of others a lot more than adult women do, but there was still something strange about it."

Jenna picked up a pretzel and rolled it between her fingers. "I guess you have a point. If you ask me, though, there was something other than sex going on."

"I agree, although it was odd how Holly was just standing there staring at Jessie and Nathan when I found them making out."

"Even odder than Jessie and Nathan hooking up in the first place. I wonder if Jessie ever told Brett what she'd done."

"You think she would?" Tj asked.

"She might have. I know Dennis and I decided to come clean about all the little white lies we'd told each other during our dating years before we got married. It led to a huge fight, but it did give us a clean slate on which to build our marriage."

Tj nibbled on the end of a carrot she'd snagged from the salad bar. The tacos were good, but they hadn't really stuck with her. Maybe she'd order a slice of Rob's pizza if the girls were going to be content to play video games until it was time to pick up Ashley and Kristi.

"The fact that Samantha is in town digging around is certainly going to make for an interesting reunion," Tj said. "If we even have one. Roy told me Mia and Jada both decided not to come after their interviews."

"Really? That's too bad. I was looking forward to catching up with them."

"Yeah, me too. They both live such interesting lives. I heard Mia's going to have a starring role in the next J. R. Morgan film."

"That's huge."

"People are already talking about an Academy Award. I can see why she wants to distance herself from this whole murder investigation. Publicity like that could only hurt her career, even if she's totally innocent."

"Yeah, if I were her I would probably avoid Serenity too, at least while the *Second Look* people are here. Did Samantha Colton have a cameraman with her when she interviewed you?"

"No, but I'm betting there's one on the way. They usually film the interviews." Tj hadn't considered the cameraman angle. but now that Jenna mentioned it, it was odd that Samantha didn't film their interview.

"The real problem I have with the series is they're known for solving cold cases, and they often do, but they even air the ones they don't close," Jenna pointed out. "When they leave things open everyone comes off looking like a possible killer, when the reality is, every person they talk to could very well be innocent. I know why Mia decided to stay away. I certainly wouldn't want Colton to cast suspicion on me and then fail to identify the killer, leaving everyone wondering. Plus, who knows what other dirty laundry she might come across in the process of her investigation."

"I feel the same way. I didn't do anything wrong, and I don't remember having any big secrets at the time of Holly's death, but I still have a knot in my stomach when I think about her turning her sights on my possible motive for killing Holly."

"Like the fact that you threatened to pull her hair out by the roots if you found out she cheated to win the homecoming queen title?" Jenna laughed.

"Yeah. Stuff like that."

"I really wouldn't worry about it," Jenna said. "Colton is just fishing. She's good at using what she does know to create a plausible story. Based on what you've told me, her strongest suspect is Brett, but if you think about it, why would Brett invite a bunch of people over to his house and then drug them if he was planning to kill Holly? The whole thing makes no sense."

"Yeah, I guess it doesn't. But I can't imagine how the others are going to react to the news that *Second Look* is in town investigating the murder after all these years."

"It's certainly going to be an interesting week," Jenna commented. "I, for one, refuse to let the investigation mar the only vacation Dennis and I have been able to take in over a year."

"I booked the two of you our best cabin, right on the water, for Thursday through Sunday," Tj confirmed.

"I can't wait. It's been so long since we've had any time alone. Did Hunter get the whole weekend off?"

"We both have to work Thursday, but we have Friday through Sunday off. I booked us the cabin next to yours for Thursday through Saturday night. I know it seems silly because I live in a big house that sits on the same plot of land as the cabin I reserved, but somehow living with your father, grandfather, and sisters cuts into the romance of the whole thing."

"We're going to have so much fun," Jenna said with excitement. "It'll be like the old days."

"I hope so." Tj tried to smile, but she was having a hard time shaking the sense of dread that felt more like a premonition. "Do you remember Rebecca Heins?"

"Yeah. She was a year behind us. She works over at Tiz the Season now."

"Roy told me that she came into the sheriff's office and gave some sort of a statement which has not been made public. I went by to ask her about it and she said that she'd get in touch with me at a better time but she is totally ignoring my calls and texts."

"I suppose you can go back by Tiz the Season and talk to her," Jenna suggested.

"I might. I was trying to let her set the pace. I mean she doesn't have to talk to me, and if I push too hard she might decide not to, but I have to say I am curious. She said she saw something that no one knows she saw. I don't suppose it is something that directly leads to the killer or the deputies would have used the information to make and arrest ten years ago, but I am curious."

"Me too. Let me know if she eventually fills you in. Right now I'm going to go check on the girls," Jenna informed Tj.

Tj looked down at her phone to check her messages after Jenna walked away. The thing about cell phones is that they made you feel like you were *on* twenty-four hours a day. She knew she could ignore her messages, texts, and emails, and at times she did, but when she did choose to ignore her phone for extended periods of time, she inevitably missed something important, which would make her vow to check in more often.

"Tj," a voice said from behind her.

Tj turned around. "Jessie." She stood up and hugged her. "I didn't know you were in town."

"We decided to come a few days early to make it more of a vacation. While that seemed like a good idea at the time, now I wish we hadn't come at all."

"Please sit down," Tj said. "I take it you've spoken to Samantha Colton?"

"Yes, I've had a chat with the she-wolf. I have no idea how she even knew we were in town early. We hadn't told anyone, but somehow she managed to track us down. She's talking to Brett right now and he isn't happy about it."

"She spoke to me today," Tj told Jessie. "And I know she spoke to Dalton and a few of the others. It seems she's making a point of tracking down everyone who was at the party. I'm afraid speaking to her isn't a pleasant experience; she's pretty aggressive about getting to the heart of the matter. I had the impression she'd already spoken to you."

"Me?" Jessie asked, surprised. "I'd never met or spoken to the woman prior to her showing up at the cabin we rented an hour ago."

"You rented a cabin? I thought you were staying at the resort."

"We were, but then we decided that everyone from our class was going to be staying at the resort and we wanted more privacy." Jessie lowered her voice. "Between you and me, Brett and I have been going through a rough patch. We thought a little privacy was in order while we tried to work through things. I'm afraid this whole reopening of the murder investigation is going to put Brett over the top. In fact, I'm sure once he manages to get rid of that woman he'll want to leave and skip the reunion altogether. I barely managed to talk him into coming in the first place."

Tj was sorry to hear Brett and Jessie were having problems. They'd seemed like the perfect couple when they were all in high school.

"I have to wonder who might have brought Holly's murder to the attention of *Second Look* in the first place," Tj said. "I've seen the show, and usually they do an investigation based on new evidence provided by someone familiar with the case who requests that they take a second look. Don't be mad, but I know you were Holly's best friend. I thought you might've been the one who got the ball rolling which is why I speculated that you'd already spoken to Samantha."

"Me?" Jessie looked shocked. "No way. I've spent the past ten years trying to forget that horrible night. Why would I want to dredge it up again?"

"I hadn't thought about it that way. I don't suppose you have any theories as to who might have been responsible for Holly's death?" Tj asked.

A strange look came over Jessie's face. "Holly wasn't the sweet, innocent thing everyone thought she was. She had secrets. Big ones. In my opinion, there are at least a half dozen people who would have been much better off with her dead. I don't have proof that any of the people who come to mind are responsible for her death, but I'll admit I wasn't entirely shocked when they found her body."

Tj frowned. "What do you mean? What secrets?"

"I really shouldn't say. Given the circumstances, I wouldn't want to cast suspicion on anyone. What's done is done and it's best to move on." Jessie looked toward the bar. "Is that Jenna Henderson?"

"Jenna Elston now, but yes."

"I'm really too tired to make small talk, so I think I'll split before she comes back. Tell her I said hi. If we don't end up leaving when Brett finishes with his interview, we can catch up later."

Tj watched Jessie hurry away. If Jessie hadn't instigated the investigation and hadn't provided Samantha with the information she had, who did? The only other person who would have known what had gone on was Nathan. Perhaps it was time to track him down. She didn't have Nathan's cell phone number but she had Bookman's home number and she knew Nathan was staying with his fellow novelist. Unfortunately, Bookman didn't answer his phone and Tj didn't think that the questions she had for Nathan were the sort of thing one would leave in a message, so she simply hung up. Chances are he'd be at the decorating party the next day and she could talk to him then.

CHAPTER 7

When Tj finally got the girls home, it was time to get them ready for bed. Hunter had mentioned stopping by that evening, so she built a fire in the living room and put soft jazz on the stereo. Her grandpa was in his room watching television and her dad was out for the evening with Rosalie. It was nice to spend a few minutes with just the animals for company while she waited for Hunter to arrive. Her life had been so hectic lately that she hadn't had any time to simply unwind and sit with her own thoughts.

The sound of the rain hitting the side of the house could be heard over the soft music. It had rained steadily for most of the day and Tj knew that if the amount of precipitation they'd already seen continued into the following day there would be flooding along the streams and rivers in the area. Although the resort was nestled on the lakeshore, the only flooding they usually had to deal with was from the smaller seasonal streams that tended to dry up over the summer.

Tj pulled an afghan over her legs, one her grandmother had crocheted right before she died. Maggie had loved to nurture her home and her family, and she'd added personal touches to every room of the house. There was still a quilt on

Tj's bed that her grandmother had hand sewn, and the hand-painted planter boxes on the back deck had been her projects one summer.

Maggie had loved to cook as well as sew, and she'd maintained a garden so she could prepare her delicious meals using the freshest produce. Ben had tried to maintain the garden for a number of years, but eventually his back and his enthusiasm had given out and he'd replaced the plants with a lawn.

Tj pulled out her phone and began checking messages. She wanted to be sure Hunter hadn't left a message saying he'd be late while she was getting the girls to bed. Nothing from Hunter, but there was a text from Jenna saying that Samantha Colton had left a message on their home phone saying she wanted to meet with both her and Dennis the following day. From Jenna's text, she seemed pretty freaked out about the whole thing.

Tj didn't blame her. Neither Dennis nor Jenna had even a slight motive to want Holly dead, but the woman was brutal. Tj worried she'd say something upsetting to Jenna, who could be sensitive at times. Tj supposed if she were the one investigating the murder she'd be doing exactly what Colton was doing and speak to everyone who had been at the party that night, but most of them really had no connection to Holly, nor would they have motives for wanting her dead.

Tj thought back to what Jessie had said. *At least a half dozen people were better off with her dead.* A bold statement coming from Holly's best friend. Was it possible their strange relationship was based on something other than affection and friendship? Could Jessie have been one of the people she'd referred to?

The more Tj thought about everything she'd learned that day, the more certain she was that lives could very well be destroyed by Colton's digging into Holly's murder. Yes, there was a killer responsible for a young girl's death, and yes, that person should be brought to justice, but what of the innocent bystanders who would have their secrets revealed and dirty laundry aired in the process of tracking down that truth?

Tj texted Jenna back instead of calling, figuring if Jenna was still awake she'd appreciate the sympathy, and if she'd gone to bed Tj wouldn't wake her. Jenna immediately responded thanking her for the encouragement. Tj knew her best friend would most likely lay awake the entire night trying to anticipate what the reporter might ask her.

Tj yawned as the stress from the day began to leave her body and the relaxing effect of the fire and the soft music lulled her toward sleep. If Hunter didn't show up soon, he'd find her asleep on the sofa. Chances were he'd gotten held up at the hospital and she was forcing herself to stay awake for nothing. She was about to call him to see if he was on his way when her phone rang. The fact that he was calling her indicated she'd be spending the remainder of the evening with only Echo and Cuervo as she'd predicted.

"Hey," she answered.

"I'm still at the hospital."

"I figured."

"We've had a rash of auto accidents today with all the rain. The last one was bad. She didn't make it."

"Oh, no. Was it anyone I know?"

"It was Samantha Colton."

Tj's heart stopped. "Samantha Colton, the woman I spoke to just this afternoon?"

"I'm afraid so."

"What happened?" Tj asked.

"She was on Old Sawmill Road, which, as you know, is very windy and has steep drop-offs. It appears she swerved to avoid something and ended up rolling down a hill and hitting a tree. There's also the possibility that she simply misread the road. It happens on nights like this, when the weather is bad and visitors to our area don't know the roads."

Tj stared into the fire. It crackled and snapped merrily as jazz played in the background. Somehow the setting seemed all wrong for the conversation.

"When did the accident occur?"

"She was brought in an hour ago. I think emergency personnel showed up pretty quickly because she had one of those alert systems in her vehicle. If I had to guess, the accident occurred no more than two hours ago. Probably less."

"You don't think—" Tj stopped herself, thinking rapidly. She had been home for maybe ninety minutes. It had been at least three hours since she'd spoken to Jessie at Rob's. She'd mentioned Brett was upset. The question was, how upset?

"That she dug too deep and someone intentionally ran her off the road? The thought crossed my mind. I spoke to one of the guys who brought her in and he said there were no obvious signs of there being a second vehicle involved in the accident. It was dark and raining, so it would've been hard to tell exactly what occurred. I imagine we'll know more after the vehicle is recovered."

Tj tucked her legs up under her body as she tried to make sense of everything. If the accident was intentional, the person who caused it must've been following Samantha. But from where? And where was she heading on that road during a storm? The more Tj thought about it, the more convinced she became that this was no accident. It didn't make sense for her to be on that road in the first place. Other than providing access to the handful of houses out there, it was rarely used now that they'd built the new highway.

"Have you spoken to Roy?" Tj asked.

"Briefly. He was as stumped as I was as to why she'd even be out there, but he was going to see what he could dig up. I'm sure we'll know more tomorrow."

Tj stared into the fire. Hunter sounded tired.

"I know we planned to get together, but I really should go home. It's late and I'm exhausted. Besides, Grandpa was in one of his moods when I left for work. I want to be sure he took his meds and ate the food I left for him rather than the crap he tends to eat when he thinks I'm too busy to notice."

"He still fighting doctor's orders?" Tj asked.

Hunter sighed. "He's doing better than he was, but it seems like it's always a struggle. I know he wants to feel better, but he seems unwilling to do what he needs to do in order to really get past this. He's supposed to be on a very restricted diet, and I make sure he has all the healthy food he wants, but I still find him sneaking around behind my back."

"It sounds like you're talking about a child rather than a grandparent," Tj pointed out.

"There are times I definitely feel like he's the child and I'm the parent. I had to work late the other night, so I left everything he would need to have a healthy meal in the refrigerator. When I came home I found a pizza box in the trash and the food I had made for him was exactly where I'd left it."

"I'm sorry. I know the situation frustrates you. Maybe I can talk to him."

Hunter sighed. "Yeah, he seems to listen to you. He certainly isn't listening to me. I'm being paged. I'll talk to you tomorrow."

"Okay. I love you."

"I love you too."

Tj felt bad for Hunter and for Jake. She knew the doctor in Hunter made him want Jake to stick to his diet all the time, but she also understood Jake's need to cheat and do things his own way every now and then. Hunter really did tend to treat Jake like a child since his stroke, but the reality was that Jake was not only an adult who was used to making his own decisions but a retired doctor capable of understanding the effects of his behavior. It would be hard for him to have someone decide that he was no longer capable of making decisions for himself after doing just that for eighty years.

But Hunter loved Jake, and he wasn't ready to let him go. Tj knew in Hunter's mind, a slice of pizza equated to less time with the man who meant so much to him.

Tj would do what she could. She'd worked out an agreement with Jake over his physical therapy sessions. She agreed to seriously consider making her arms-length relationship with Hunter a bit more official if he agreed to go to his therapy sessions and do as his therapist ordered. At that time, she'd thought the purpose of the agreement was to help Jake, but the reality was that Jake's stubbornness had really helped her to admit her feelings for Hunter. On the surface, agreeing to make a commitment to someone's grandson in exchange for them agreeing to the medical treatment they needed had seemed ridiculous, but in retrospect Jake had simply provided a means for Tj to do what she was pretty sure she already wanted to do.

Tj sent a text to Jenna. There was no use her worrying all night about an interview that was never going to happen.

No need to stress over your interview tomorrow. There isn't going to be one.

Why not?

Colton was in an accident. She's dead.

What? When?

A few hours ago. I just got off the phone with Hunter.

Tj's phone rang as she waited for Jenna to text back. She supposed she should have just called her friend in the first place.

"What happened?" Jenna asked.

Tj shared what she knew, which wasn't a lot. She also gave her opinion that the accident might not have been an accident at all.

"Dennis and I were talking about Samantha Colton earlier, after we learned she wanted to speak with both of us. He told me he'd spoken to Dalton, who warned him that she was going to ruin lives and needed to be dealt with."

"You don't think that Dalton?"

Jenna let out a long breath. "No. I don't know. Maybe."

"After my own interview with the barracuda I can confirm that the woman had a way of pushing buttons but I can't believe Dalton would actually follow through with his threat."

"Yeah, I suppose you're right. It's just that when you told me the woman was dead my initial reaction was relief and that isn't me at all. Add to that the fact that I don't really have any big dark secrets and I was being interviewed as a witness and not a suspect. I can't imagine how stressed out the actual suspects might be."

"The woman certainly has stirred up some strong emotions in the community. I won't be a bit surprised to find out that her accident wasn't an accident after all."

CHAPTER 8

Wednesday, October 28

"Pancakes?" Ben asked when Tj came down the stairs for a cup of coffee. "Schools are closed due to the flooding."

"I'd love some." Tj walked across the room and gave her grandfather a big hug. "I saw the text from the school when I first woke up. Let me get the girls and we can all eat together."

"That'd be nice. Your dad had to run over to the lodge, but he said he'd be back in twenty minutes."

"Perfect. That will give me time to grab a quick shower."

Tj let Echo out for his morning run, then headed upstairs to wake up her sisters. She was looking forward to having breakfast with her family. It had been too long since they'd sat down and shared the first meal of the day together. Tj had been raised by her dad and grandparents after her mom had left when she was three. If there was one thing Maggie had insisted on, it was that the family have the first and the last meals of the day together. Ben continued to try to keep the custom alive by taking care of most of the cooking, but with the busy lives they all led, it seemed that more often than not everyone was on a different schedule.

After Tj woke her sisters she headed to her bathroom for her shower. Tj, Mike, and Ben all had baths adjoining their bedrooms, while the girls shared a bathroom between them. When both of her sisters needed showers before bed Tj had one of them use her bathroom, which meant the room wasn't as tidy as she liked to keep it. Making a mental note to give it a good scrubbing when she had the opportunity, she quickly showered and then dressed in warm but comfortable clothes.

After making her bed and straightening her room, Tj headed down to the kitchen. She could hear the girls talking to Ben. When Tj first found out she was going to be responsible for two young girls, she'd been concerned about how being an instant mother would affect her life. She'd been living in town in a small apartment and wasn't responsible for anyone but herself. But after the girls came to live with her, she'd decided to move back to the resort where she'd have the support of her dad and grandpa. Looking at what she'd given up and what she now had, she knew she wouldn't trade her cluttered life for anything.

"Papa said that he is going down to the valley to look at a new horse for the stable," Gracie announced when Tj walked in.

"That sounds like fun." Tj glanced at her dad. "Are you still thinking about adding to our breeding stock?"

"I am." Mike, dressed in a warm sweater and blue jeans, grinned as he answered. "We have a couple of mares who are ready to be retired. I've found them good homes with families with young children but I really need to find a couple of replacements before breeding season."

"My friend has a horse of her very own," Ashley contributed. "I wish I had a horse of my own."

"The stock at Maggie's Hideaway is working stock," Mike reminded her. "But you know you are welcome to ride with supervision anytime the horses aren't busy."

"What are you doing today, Grandpa?" Gracie asked after everyone else had shared their plans. Leave it to Gracie to make sure everyone participated in the conversation.

"I thought I'd decorate the house for Halloween." Ben turned to look at Tj. "Do you know what happened to the Halloween decorations we put up in the house last year?"

"I think they're in the attic. I'll look for them after we eat. The girls can help me bring them down."

"Can we put up the giant mummy we used for the Halloween party last year?" Ashley asked. "He was cool."

"I thought we'd put him on the front porch," Ben said. "I checked the weather forecast and it looks like it's going to rain again today but then be dry until after next weekend. Besides, the porch is covered, so there's no problem even if we get a few sprinkles. I'm going to put orange lights around the door and windows as well."

"We should string spider webs too," Ashley added. "And we can put those big rubber spiders on them. It will look spooky. I'm going to make my pumpkin extra spooky this year. Can I help you decorate?"

"I'd be happy to have the help," Ben said.

"Can Pumpkin help too?" Gracie asked.

"The more the merrier. Still no word on an owner?" Ben asked Tj.

"Not so far."

"Rosalie seems to think she's a stray," Mike confirmed. "She said she has the look of a pup that's been on the street for a while."

"I'm so glad we found her so she can have a forever home," Gracie declared.

Tj glanced at her dad. They hadn't discussed keeping Pumpkin on a permanent basis, but he just smiled and winked at her.

"Can we get Pumpkin a costume for Halloween?" Gracie asked.

"I'm not sure she'll want to wear a costume. She'll probably just pull it off and chew it up. Maybe we can try a hat or a special collar," Tj suggested. "I think there might be something up in the attic from when Echo was a puppy. I always wanted to dress him up, but he wanted nothing to do with it. Every time I tried to put something on him he rolled around until he got it off. I finally gave up."

"Pumpkin likes to dress up," Gracie assured me. "I put one of my shirts on her and she liked it."

"She does seem to have more patience than most puppies," Tj admitted.

"If she likes wearing a costume can we get her one?"

"We'll see," Tj answered noncommittally.

Everyone finished their meal and Tj and the girls headed up to the attic to look for the decorations, as well as the old costumes Tj remembered saving. Attics were the best places, she decided, as they sorted through boxes filled with remnants from experiences she had all but forgotten.

"Look at all these old books." Tj pulled a pile of mysteries out of the carton in front of her. "These used to belong to

Grandma Maggie, and then she gave them to me. I bet they'd be just about perfect for you," Tj said to Ashley.

Ashley shrugged. "I like to read. I guess I can take a few down and try them."

"Are there any books that would be perfect for me?" Gracie asked.

"I'm pretty sure I saved the set of Raggedy Ann books Papa found at a garage sale. They aren't in this box, but we can keep looking."

"Is this your cheerleading uniform?" Ashley asked after opening another box.

Tj nodded. "I was a cheerleader for all four years of high school, so there should be four uniforms in there. I'm not sure why we thought we needed a new uniform every year, but we did."

"I want to be a cheerleader," Ashley decided.

Tj was surprised to hear that. It didn't seem like Ashley was in to typical girly stuff.

"The fact that you're taking dance will help you," Tj informed her sister. "In order to be on the cheer squad these days you have to be well versed in gymnastics. It's fun, though. You make good friends and you get to go with the team to all the away games."

"Was Dr. Hunter on the football team?" Gracie asked.

"He was," Tj said.

"Did you smooch on the backseat of the bus?" Ashley giggled.

"We might have," Tj admitted.

"Ewww," Gracie said as she buried her head in her arms.

Tj laughed. "Just wait a few years. You won't think it's so ewww."

Tj noticed Ashley hadn't parroted her younger sister's sentiments. She was growing up so fast. It wouldn't be long at all before she was sneaking kisses in the backseat of the team bus.

"Is this your yearbook?" Ashley held up the book from her senior year.

"Yes."

"Is the girl who died in here?"

"Yes. There's a special page dedicated to her in the middle of the book."

Ashley opened the book as Pumpkin wrestled around with Echo on the floor and Midnight hissed at them from atop a trunk.

"She was really pretty," Ashley said. "It's so sad she died."

"She *was* pretty but not always all that nice."

Holly enjoyed her status as one of the popular girls of the high school and wasn't afraid to tear other people down if it meant building herself up. Until now Tj had forgotten how mean she could be if she felt threatened by those she considered to be on a lower social rung than she. Tj thought about what Chantel had said, and Lexi and the bullying she had fallen victim to. Could the killer be one of the girls Holly had bullied? Several of the girls at the party that night had been Holly's victim at one time or another. Maybe the bullying angle would be worth considering.

"Look at Pumpkin," Gracie squealed.

Pumpkin was lying patiently on the floor with an orange and black witch hat on her head. Tj pulled her cell out of her pocket and snapped a photo. Pumpkin really was the perfect puppy for Gracie, calm and patient. Tj hoped her owner wouldn't show up at the eleventh hour. Gracie would be crushed.

"I think these are the boxes Grandpa wants us to bring down," Ashley said after setting the yearbook aside.

"It looks like it. But only carry boxes you can pick up comfortably. Leave the heavy ones for me."

Each of the girls picked up a box and headed down the stairs. They'd have the best decorated house in town.

"I never remember the *u*," Gracie whined later that morning. Tj had been helping her to study for the spelling bee and the word had been glamour.

"The *u* is tricky," Tj admitted. "It sounds like it should be *glam* followed by *or*. Don't worry. We'll keep practicing until you know it like the back of your hand."

"What does that mean anyway?" Gracie asked. "The back of your hand. Why would I know the back of my hand?"

"It's just a saying. To be honest, I have no idea where it came from."

"Let's Google it," Gracie suggested.

"Good idea. What did we ever do before we had Google?"

"We just didn't know stuff."

Gracie giggled as Pumpkin jumped up onto her bed and began licking her face. Gracie loved animals and they loved her. Tj had really thought Crissy would abandon her when Pumpkin made herself at home on Gracie's bed, but the cat seemed unwilling to give up her spot, so she was tolerating the dog.

Tj typed the phrase into her laptop. "There are a bunch of answers. The most common is that when you know something well you know it like the back of your hand because you know your hand well."

"That's dumb," Gracie commented.

"I have to agree. It's not like I spend a lot of time looking at the back of my hand. Let's move on to the next word: *proximity*. The dog was in the proximity of the doghouse."

"P-r-o-x-i-m-i-t-y," Gracie said. "Proximity."

"Very good. You really do know most of these words."

"Grandpa has been helping me, but the really hard words are on the last page."

Tj turned to the last page. "*Articulate*? Are you sure you have the second-grade list? These words seem hard for second grade. Heck, they seem hard for any grade."

"They're supposed to be hard," Gracie insisted. "If they weren't, everyone could spell them and it wouldn't be any big deal to be the spelling champion."

"I guess that's true." Tj continued to study the list. There were several words she was pretty sure she wouldn't be able to spell herself without the help of spell-check. There'd been a debate going on in the English department as to whether computers and smartphones weren't actually making people dumber. With all the knowledge easily accessed on the internet, Tj thought people were actually becoming smarter, but she could see that with each new generation skills such as spelling and handwriting might decline.

"Most of the time the words on the very last page aren't used, but you need to know them just in case," Gracie informed her. "There's a girl in my class who told me that her parents make her study for three hours every day. They go through the dictionary and pick out random words. Any words. If she can spell them all she gets some time to hang out with her friends on the weekend; if she misses them she has to study on the weekend."

Tj frowned. "That's crazy. It's just a spelling bee."

"Trisha's parents are very ambitious and tenacious."

Tj laughed. "Tenacious? Where did you learn a word like that?"

"That's how Trisha describes her parents. Trisha knows how to spell tenacious. I don't think I have a chance of winning, but I thought it would be fun to try."

"As long as you're having fun I'm all for it, but I don't want you to forget to be a kid."

"I won't. Can we do some more words?"

Tj looked out the window. It was still raining. The girls wouldn't be able to go out, making it a good day to study, but she had a long list of errands waiting for her.

"I think we've studied enough for today," Tj said. "We can work on your words more tomorrow."

"Okay."

"How about a snack?" Tj asked.

"Can Pumpkin have a snack?"

"Absolutely."

Tj settled Gracie in the kitchen and went to find Ashley. The fact that Trisha's parents were *so* driven really bothered her. Sure, academic achievement was important. Learning to be a good student made all the difference in the options you had as you approached adulthood. But kids needed to be kids as well. They needed to play outdoors and watch cartoons and do kidlike things while they were young enough to appreciate their simplicity.

She supposed Trisha's parents had the right to raise their daughter however they saw fit. She might not agree with their methods, but there really wasn't a thing she could do about it. Navigating parenthood was a difficult task. One wrong move and...Tj didn't want to think about that. She'd just gotten to the point where she wasn't second-guessing every decision she made.

"It's time to turn off the television," Tj said to Ashley, who was watching a popular sitcom on TV.

"Just a few more minutes."

"You can finish this program and then we need to find another activity. You know the rule about TV time."

"I know, but it's raining. We can't go outside and there isn't anything to do."

"I just don't want your brain to rot."

"That wouldn't really happen. Can Kristi come over?"

"It depends. I need to go into town in a while to help Dr. Hunter decorate the gym for the homecoming dance. Where's Papa?"

"He went into town. I think he was going to meet up with Rosalie. Are they going to get married?"

Good question.

"I don't know," Tj answered. "I guess Papa will tell us if he decides to take that step. Did Grandpa go up to his room?"

"He said he wasn't feeling well. His back has been bothering him a lot lately."

"I noticed that too. I'll check on him, but I don't think it's a good idea to have company if Papa and I won't be here and Grandpa doesn't feel well."

"But it's *so* boring. Can we go over to Kristi's?"

Tj realized that if Ben wasn't feeling well it might not be a bad idea to get the girls out of the house, but she knew Jenna and Dennis were both working, so Jenna's sister, Bren, was babysitting. Maybe Kyle would welcome some company.

"Kristi and Kari are over at Bren's and I hate to ask her to watch two more kids, but maybe Uncle Kyle is home."

Ashley grinned. "Can we call him?"

"Yeah, I'll call him."

CHAPTER 9

Luckily, Kyle was home and happy not only to have Ashley and Gracie over for the afternoon but Echo and Pumpkin as well. Kyle often said he got lonely living in his great big house since his mom moved out and his ward, Annabeth, had been accepted into a boarding school that catered to students in need of an accelerated learning environment. Annabeth still came home during the summer and school holidays, but Kyle was usually up for some kid time while she was away.

"Thanks for letting the girls hang out for a while," Tj said after Kyle ushered the girls inside.

"I'm happy to have them and I wanted to meet Pumpkin." Kyle knelt down on the floor to pet the rambunctious puppy. "Gracie told me all about her."

"You talked to Gracie?"

"She called to tell me about the spelling bee and mentioned that she found the puppy."

Tj watched as Kyle's dog Trooper greeted Echo. One thing was for certain: with two wound-up grade-schoolers and three dogs, Kyle wasn't going to be bored that afternoon.

"Did you hear about the accident on Old Sawmill Road last night?"

"No. What happened?"

Tj looked over at the girls, who were watching them with interest.

"I have a bunch of new video games," Kyle announced. "Would you like to check them out? Annabeth even has one about being a fashion designer."

"That sounds dope," Ashley said.

Kyle turned to Tj. "If you have a minute, I can get the girls settled and then we can chat."

"Sure, I can be a few minutes late."

Tj called Hunter while Kyle headed toward the den with her sisters. During the two years since Kyle had inherited the house from Zachary he'd undertaken a major renovation. The lakeside estate no longer resembled the run-down mansion Tj had visited as a teen. While the house had always seemed so dark and dreary when Zachary lived there, Kyle had added additional windows and opened it up so the lake and surrounding forest felt as if it were part of the structure itself. The house was located on an isolated bay surrounded with old growth pines providing a feeling of both beauty and isolation.

"So what's up?" Kyle asked when he returned to the living room, where Tj had taken a seat on one of the three sofas in the room.

Tj filled him in on everything she'd learned since her meeting with Samantha Colton the previous afternoon. It certainly seemed like more than twenty-four hours had passed since the domineering woman sat in her office and made her doubt everything she previously believed to be true.

"It sounds like her interview technique could have used some finessing," Kyle commented.

"She approached the task like she was orchestrating a military attack. While the accident could have been just that, an accident, I'd be willing to bet Holly's killer is still in the area and wanted to make sure he or she wasn't found out."

"Maybe," Kyle responded. "Colton might've spooked someone who didn't want their secrets leaked, but that doesn't necessarily mean the same person who killed Holly killed her. It sounds like she dug up new dirt on pretty much everyone there that night. If she intended to air all that information as a ratings booster, anyone involved might have wanted her dead."

Jessie might not have wanted Brett to know, even now, that she had cheated on him with Nathan, and Nathan might've wanted that fact kept secret as well. Samantha Colton had speculated that Jessie and Holly had been involved in a romantic relationship, and even if it wasn't true, Tj doubted Jessie would want that aired on national television. Likewise, Dalton might not welcome the comparison of his infatuation with Holly to that of a stalker.

"You're right," Tj realized. "Holly's killer had the largest stake in wanting Samantha Colton gone, but there are plenty of people who'll sleep more soundly tonight knowing she isn't about to expose their deep, dark secrets to the world."

"Did *Second Look* send a cameraman along with Colton?" Kyle asked.

"She didn't bring one with her when she came to talk to me, and no one else has mentioned a cameraman, but I assume she had one somewhere in the wings. I mean, it's a television show. A cameraman would be essential."

"Maybe someone should track down this person and see what they know. Colton clearly made some enemies doing what she does. It's even possible someone from another cold case she was working on followed her to Paradise Lake with the intention of killing her. That's what I would do if I wanted someone like her dead."

"Come again?"

Kyle adjusted his position on the sofa so he was looking directly at Tj. "Think of it this way: The woman dies under mysterious circumstances shortly after interviewing a bunch of people about a ten-year-old murder. If Colton really was run off the road intentionally, the obvious conclusion is that someone involved in the current case killed her to prevent her from finding out the truth or, as we surmised, from leaking their secrets. And that may be where you find your murderer. But if I wanted to kill Colton, running her off the road shortly after she spoke to me would make me an obvious suspect. I'd wait until she moved on to the next town, the next cold case, follow her, and do the deed there. No one would be looking at individuals involved in the last story she researched or the next one she planned to research. It really is the smarter way to go about carrying out a murder."

"You're a scary man, Kyle Donovan."

He smiled and shrugged.

"But you aren't wrong. We would need to look at individuals involved in this case as well as individuals involved in other cases she was working on. Specifically, those that haven't aired yet. I'll suggest to Roy that he should call the *Second Look* people to see if he can get that information."

"We can get information about Samantha Colton's past cases online," Kyle suggested. "The television show has a calendar of both past and future episodes. Maybe we can narrow it down and then call Roy. I bet the poor guy is swamped."

"I'm supposed to meet Hunter at the decorating party but this seems more important. I'll text him and let him know I'll be late while you pull up the website."

Kyle pulled up the site while Tj texted Hunter.

"That's interesting," Kyle commented.

"What's interesting?"

"Each episode listed gives a brief description of the murder as well as the identity of the reporting team who covered the murder. For those episodes which have already aired it also describes the outcome of the investigation."

Tj looked over Kyle's shoulder.

"See here," Kyle continued. "Last week's episode was a rerun, so the last new episode to air was two weeks ago. The murder involved a young mother in Kansas. The investigating team are identified as Carl Miller and Bianca Tillman."

"So?"

"So if you look back through the episode descriptions you will find that there is always a team of reporters, yet so far no one seems to have spoken to anyone other than Samantha Colton."

"Yeah, I guess that is odd. Can you find the last case she researched?"

Kyle flipped through the episodes. "The last case I can find where Samantha Colton is listed as a reporter is three months ago. She was teamed with a man named Frank Ralston. They investigated the murder of a college student." Kyle paused as he scanned down. "It looks like she was having an affair with one of her professors. Local police were sure the professor killed her, but it turned out it was really another student who had been involved with the same professor the previous year."

"How often do most of the reporters come up in the rotation?" Tj asked.

Kyle opened the webpage for the other recent episodes and jotted down the names of the reporters. "It looks like there are eight teams of reporters which means if you take into account the weeks when there are reruns or the show doesn't air for whatever reason, three months between episodes isn't really all that far off. Still in every case there is a team, so where is the second reporter."

"Did Samantha team up with Frank Rolston every time?"

"I'm not sure. I'll keep digging and see what I can find out."

Tj looked at her watch. She was going to be *very* late helping with the decorating, but this was more immediately important. "I should call Roy. If there is a second reporter, he should know about it and if there isn't a second reporter he should be made aware that covering a case alone is not the norm. Plus, how can you have a show without a cameraman? The whole thing seems odd."

"Okay, you call Roy and I'll keep looking."

Tj pulled out her cell and dialed the number to Roy's private cell.

"Hey, Roy," Tj greeted when he answered his phone.

"Hey, Tj. What's up?"

She filled him in on her discussion with Kyle.

"I don't really watch the show and wasn't aware that there should be a reporting team but it did occur to me that there should be a cameraman. I spent a good part of the morning trying to find him with zero success," Roy informed her. "I haven't even figured out where Ms. Colton was staying. Not a single lodging in the area has any information on her. And that isn't even the strangest thing I found out."

"What's the strangest thing you found out?"

"I called the *Second Look* offices to inform them about the accident and find out where she was staying and whether she had anyone with her. It took me three phone calls to get through to the right person, but when I did finally track that person down, he told me that while Samantha Colton used to be a reporter for them she no longer works for them."

"What? That makes no sense? If she no longer works for them why was she running around town interviewing everyone?"

"The man I spoke to said that the Holly Riverton case was brought to their attention two months ago but they'd decided to pass on it. Samantha quit shortly after that. If Samantha Colton was in town asking questions, she was doing it on her own."

"Didn't you check her out when she contacted you about talking to us?" Tj asked.

Roy sighed. "Not as much as I should have. She had identification that proved she worked for *Second Look*, and she sounded like she knew what she was talking about. Her story about doing a feature for the show seemed reasonable."

"Why would this woman come to Paradise Lake to investigate a murder she hadn't been assigned to?"

"The man I spoke to had no idea."

"Wow." Tj let out a long breath. "This was already pretty complicated, but now..."

"Yeah, the whole thing just keeps getting odder and odder."

Tj glanced at Kyle who was looking at her. She made a motion to let him know she'd fill him in when she completed her call.

"Did Samantha have any personal possessions with her when she had her accident? A laptop or cell phone perhaps?"

"We didn't find her laptop but the crime scene guys did find her phone. I haven't had a chance to go through it yet, but I will. To be honest, I've been swamped. I really could use some help."

"Did you call the county office?" Tj asked.

"I did. They said they'd try to find someone to send over, but it didn't sound promising. That big poker tournament is going on over at the casinos and there are a million people in town. Sounds like they're pretty busy."

"The gang and I will do what we can," Tj offered.

"Thanks. I was counting on that. I'll see if I can find out about a computer and call you back. I do know there wasn't anything in the car other than her purse which is where we found her phone, so unless we can figure out where she was staying..."

"Check her purse for a small notebook," Tj suggested. "She was jotting down notes the entire time I was talking to her. Maybe everything we need to know is inside. If nothing else, her notes should provide us with a suspect list."

After Tj hung up she filled Kyle in on her conversation with Roy.

"That's nuts. How could this have even happened? It seems like the first thing Roy would have done was check to verify that the woman was investigating on behalf of *Second Look*."

"You know I love Roy. He is a wonderful and caring man

who I have known most of my life. But to be honest he's only a so-so cop. Add that to the fact that he's alone since Dylan left and Tim was arrested with only the temporary help the main office sees fit to send, and I can honestly understand how the fact that Samantha no longer worked for *Second Look* could have slipped through the cracks."

"Okay so if he doesn't have help let's help him," Kyle suggested. "Where should we start?"

"If she was working on her own there most likely isn't a cameraman to find. Roy is going to check her phone and notebook. Maybe we should try to find out where she was staying. I really need to get to the decorating party but maybe you can use your techy know-how to check her credit card purchases or something."

"Yeah, okay. I'll see what I can find out. We'll compare notes once you are finished decorating."

CHAPTER 10

Tj headed to the decorating party. She hated to leave Kyle to investigate Samantha's movements the last few days on his own but she'd promised Hunter she'd meet him there and she knew several of the *suspects* would be there. Tj was operating under the assumption that everyone connected to the party the night of Holly's murder was fair game for Samantha Colton's intensive investigative campaign and therefore a suspect in her possible murder.

Tj drove slowly through town on her way to the high school. The orange and white twinkle lights that had been strung in all the trees along the main drag sparkled as they reflected off the wet pavement.

Hopefully tomorrow would be sunny and warm as predicted, allowing the football field time to dry out before the big game on Friday. Serenity High School had a good team this year, creating a buzz among local football fans that this could be the year the team made it all the way to the state finals.

The rain had slowed to an occasional drizzle and the areas where seasonal streams had overflowed onto the nearby roadways were already beginning to recede. Because the schools were scheduled to be closed for Nevada Day on Friday, tomorrow was Tj's best opportunity to carry out the plan she'd developed with Chantel to lessen Lexi's embarrassment over the shower video.

Before heading to the gym, Tj made a quick stop at her office to call the girls who'd offered to help pull off their plan. Tj was a popular teacher, and Lexi a genuinely sweet girl, so she had no problem convincing the girls on her team to help. If things went as planned, the sting from the video would be minimized, allowing Lexi to return to school with her head held high.

She was about to call the last name on her list when her phone rang.

"Hey, Roy. What's up?"

"I located that little notebook you were talking about. Looks like Ms. Colton wrote in a self-made shorthand, but I did manage to decipher a few things. She ranked her suspects based on the likelihood that they killed Holly."

"Okay so what are the rankings?"

"Brett Conrad is number one, followed by Mackenzie Paulson, Jessie Baldwin, Jada Jenkins, and you."

"Terrific."

"Mia Monroe was sixth, but her name was crossed off."

"Colton mentioned she'd changed her mind about Mia as a suspect. Who's seventh?"

"Dalton Fowler, followed by Doreen Sullwold, Nathan Fullerton, and Vicki Davis."

"I spoke to Doreen Sullwold at the costume store the other day. She said that she and Vicki Davis came to the party together and then left together. Vicki spent the night with

Doreen so we can cross both of them off the list. Most of the others should be here other than Jada. I'll mingle and see what I can find out. Did you manage to find out who Colton spoke to prior to her accident?"

"The number was blocked."

"That's unfortunate. By the way, did you find any evidence explaining why Colton's car swerved off the road?"

"There's a suspicious dent on the left front fender of her vehicle that doesn't look to have been caused by the impact with the tree. The crime scene guys are still looking at it, but the evidence is inconclusive at this point."

"Okay, but at this point I'm going to operate on the assumption she was murdered. The woman ruffled a lot of feathers. Call or text if you get anything else."

"Will do."

After Tj had called all the students she needed to speak to regarding her plan to help Lexi, she headed over to the gym where the homecoming dance was to be held. The merry band of volunteers seemed to have everything well in hand.

"Glad you made it." Hunter kissed her on the cheek.

"It looks like things are almost finished."

"Not quite, but we're making good progress. We should be able to wrap everything up in a couple of hours. Want to grab some dinner when we're done?"

"I have the girls, and we have a new twist to the case, so maybe a sleuthing dinner with the gang? Kyle is on board, and I'm going to ask Jenna if she and Dennis want to meet with us as well. I'm thinking Rob's, so the kids can play video games while we talk."

"Not exactly the romantic dinner I was hoping for, but I'm game."

"You don't seem to actually need my help, so I'm going to mingle," Tj informed Hunter.

"By mingle do you mean investigate?"

"You know me so well."

Hunter returned to his task while Tj scanned the room. In addition to Hunter and Jenna, who she could speak to later and who she knew hadn't killed either Holly or Samantha Colton, there were seven other suspects in the room. Dalton Fowler had shown up with his wife, Marianne. Tj remembered Colton had interviewed Dalton on the day she died, and Marianne had indicated that the interview had upset her husband. Back in high school Dalton had been obsessed with Holly, and while his obsession could have turned to murder, Tj doubted he was the guilty party. Still, until she could prove otherwise, he would remain firmly on the suspect list.

Brett and Jessie were also in the room. Tj was surprised they hadn't left after his interview. The fact that Colton was dead wasn't widely known at this point, yet the couple were laughing and having a good time. Was it possible they knew about the accident because they had caused it?

Doreen Sullwold and Vicki Davis had both attended the party on the night Holly was murdered but unless they both lied about being together, which Tj doubted, she'd cleared them.

Mackenzie Paulson, the class valedictorian, was also there. Tj was surprised to see that she'd come to town early. Her job with NASA kept her busy most of the time, but here she was, chatting with Teddy Bolton, a local dentist who had surprised everyone when he became one after spending the majority of his high school years completely stoned. Both

Teddy and Mackenzie had been at the party the night Holly was murdered.

Tj decided to start with Mackenzie. She'd been second on Samantha's list, which was surprising, and she hadn't seen her since she'd visited Paradise three years ago.

"Mac," Tj greeted her enthusiastically.

"I was hoping to run into you." Mackenzie turned and hugged Tj. "When I saw Hunter and Jenna I thought you'd be here, but Jenna said you were dropping your girls off at a friend's. You surely haven't had children since I was here last."

"No, the girls Jenna referred to are my sisters."

Mackenzie frowned. "I thought you were an only child?"

Tj explained how Ashley and Gracie had come into her life.

"Wow. That's a lot of responsibility."

Tj laughed. "Coming from a woman with top-level clearance who's responsible for software that ensures our national security."

"A different kind of responsibility from raising children. I don't think I could do it."

"It's not so bad if you ease into it," added Teddy, who had two sons of his own.

Mackenzie looked around the room. "It's so odd to see everyone married and settled into their roles of raising families. I work a lot of hours, and when I'm not working I hang out with people from work who likewise are single and child-free. Then I come to Serenity and the main topic of conversation is soccer camp and school carnivals. I feel like I've been dropped into another dimension. I'm probably the only one from our class without a couple of rug rats."

"Hardly," Tj countered. "Brett and Jessie don't have children, and Vicki isn't married. Jada and Mia aren't coming to the reunion, but neither of them has children."

"I just spoke to Jada a week ago and she told me she'd be here."

"She was planning to attend," Tj said. "I understand she and Mia both changed their minds after speaking to Samantha Colton."

"The *Second Look* lady?"

"That's the one. Did she speak to you?"

"Yeah, she called me and asked if I was planning to be in Serenity this week. She said she was investigating Holly's murder for the show. I told her I really didn't know anything, but I agreed to meet with her. I'm seeing her tomorrow afternoon. Why would her interviews with Jada and Mia cause them to cancel their trips?"

Tj hesitated. Roy probably wanted to keep the woman's death, accidental or not, quiet until he could track down the next of kin. If Mackenzie was still expecting to meet Colton the next day, it was clear she hadn't killed her.

"Colton can be pretty brutal when it comes to digging into your past. It was clear to me that she'd done her homework and already had a list of suspects in mind before she met with any of us. From what I understand, Jada and Mia were offended by some of the accusations she made."

"I thought the woman was investigating Holly's death, not the sordid past of the alumni of Serenity High School," Teddy commented.

"She was. I mean is. It's just that she seems to consider every person who was at Brett's party that night a suspect, so she's digging around in everyone's past, looking for motives."

"Yikes. That's not going to bode so well for me," Teddy murmured.

Tj glanced at Mackenzie, who hadn't said anything but was frowning.

"Has she arranged to talk to you as well?" Tj asked Teddy.

"Yeah. Tomorrow morning. I doubt I can be of much help. I was so stoned my entire high school career I can't remember much. I know I was at the party; there are photos to prove it. But I honestly can't remember anything that happened after we were all standing around in the parking lot."

"How did you ever manage to graduate college, let alone dental school?" Mackenzie asked.

"I guess I had a few unfried brain cells," Teddy said. "Once I got clean and sober, they started working again."

"You have those pictures?" Tj asked.

"Yeah. A bunch. A couple of the cheerleaders were running around with disposable cameras at the party."

"I remember that. I'm not sure who brought them, but I do remember having my photo snapped more than once. How did you end up with the photos?"

"The cameras ended up in my backpack. I didn't notice I had them until I got home. When I saw Brett at school the next week I asked him what I should do with them. He didn't know who'd brought them, so he said I should just toss them. I had the film developed anyway. The photos were pretty bad. I'm not sure why I kept them."

"Would you mind if I take a look at them?" Tj asked.

"Sure. I'll need to dig them up, though. I'll bring them to the reception tomorrow."

"Fantastic." Tj turned to Mackenzie. "I'd love to have a chance to catch up some more. Are you in town through the weekend?"

"That's the plan, unless that reporter lady scares me off too."

"Don't worry. Next to Hunter, you were the most serious, responsible student in our class. I doubt she has anything on you."

"We all have secrets."

Tj wanted to ask Mackenzie what she meant by that, but she realized this wasn't the best place to get involved in a serious conversation. She said her goodbyes to the pair and headed over to where Brett was chatting with Dalton. Both men had already had their interviews, which moved them higher on the suspect list, at least in regard to Samantha Colton's death.

Despite the tension created by Colton and her investigation, it seemed the room was filled with positive energy. Classmates who hadn't seen one another for years were chatting happily as they strung streamers and hung old yearbook photos someone had blown up. There was a part of Tj that wanted to leave the investigating to Roy so she could join in the fun, but a bigger part wanted this increasingly complex mystery solved.

"If it isn't little Tj Jensen," Brett said as he lifted her into the air in a giant bear hug.

Tj laughed. "It's wonderful to see you. How've you been?"

He set her back down but didn't answer.

"Brett and I are both recovering from the brutal interviews we had to deal with yesterday," Dalton shared.

"Has the witch from the cold case show talked to you yet?"

"Yes, I've had the pleasure of her company," Tj answered. "She definitely isn't shy about tossing around allegations."

"Here's what I don't get," Dalton said. "The woman is supposed to be here to investigate Holly's murder, but what she's really doing is running around digging up dirt on everyone who was even remotely connected to Holly. She seems to have found a plausible motive for everyone at the party to have killed her. Even you."

Tj was less than thrilled that Samantha had been going around accusing her of murder but she supposed that was what she was doing with everyone.

"Don't worry. I told her she was totally off base," Dalton added. "If anyone had a motive to kill that tease it was me, but I didn't do it."

Tj gave Dalton a shocked look.

"Everyone knows I had it bad for Holly when we were in high school. I was in love with her, but she treated me like a toy. The bitch used to get all sorts of pleasure out of leading me on and then shutting me down at the last minute. Did you know she even came to my house on occasion in skimpy outfits to *study* when my parents weren't home? I should have told her to get lost. But even though she teased me to within an inch of sanity, I followed her around like a little puppy. God, I was pathetic."

"Don't be so hard on yourself," Brett said, patting him on the shoulder. "Holly liked to control people, and she was great at figuring out your weak spot. Once she did, she'd use it to manipulate you. She did it to Jessie all the time. I tried to tell Jessie what Holly was doing, but she wouldn't hear it.

I'm not sure who killed the witch, but I honestly think whoever it was did us all a favor."

"That seems kind of harsh," Tj said.

Brett shrugged. "I'm just saying what everyone is thinking. That girl was a user who didn't care who she hurt. Jessie and I probably wouldn't be together if Holly hadn't died."

Tj had thought the same thing, but she was surprised to hear Brett admit it himself. Him openly sharing his hatred of Holly, knowing it would throw suspicion on him, made it likely he hadn't killed either Holly or Samantha Colton. On the other hand, openly stating something you know everyone else is thinking could be a clever tactic to divert suspicion if you really are guilty.

"Jessie is waving me over," Brett said. "We'll catch up later." He walked away.

Tj looked at Dalton. "If you had to make a guess, who do you think killed Holly?"

Dalton furrowed his brow. "We're talking theoretically?" he finally asked.

"Yeah. Unless you do know who did it."

"I don't, but if I had to guess, I'd say Jada Jenkins."

Tj frowned. "Why Jada?"

"Because she was dating fellow nerd Rodney Stone senior year, and Holly was sleeping with him at the same time."

"Really? How do you know?"

"I used to follow Holly around, if you remember. I probably knew more about what she did than anyone."

Dalton had a point. He had stalked her for most of the year prior to her death.

"You were both still at Brett's party when I left," Tj said. "Do you remember if Holly was too?"

"I was pretty wasted, but I'm pretty sure she went upstairs with Jessie at some point. She definitely wasn't still downstairs when I decided to stumble home."

Jada had been involved in a serious relationship with Rodney when they were in high school. She had thrown herself into the software she developed and never married, and Tj at times wondered if Jada had really ever gotten over her messy breakup with the person she'd told everyone was the love of her life.

CHAPTER 11

After the decorating party, Tj and Hunter met Kyle and her sisters at Rob's Pizza. Dennis, Jenna, and their girls joined them shortly after. Kyle had informed Tj that they'd dropped Echo and Pumpkin off at the resort on their way to eat so she wouldn't have to worry about picking them up later.

They ordered several family-size pizzas, and Tj gave the girls money for video games, with instructions to behave and stay together. It really was too bad the main topic of conversation had to be murder. Rob had gone all out to decorate for Halloween, and it would have been nice to be able to simply enjoy the company of her friends in a warm, inviting setting, without having to worry about the high school students in the next booth overhearing the details of the two deaths Tj was now determined to solve. Thankfully, the kids were almost done with their meal, and given the weather and the late hour, it was unlikely that anyone else would occupy the space after they left.

"So did you learn any juicy tidbits when you were snooping this afternoon?" Jenna asked.

"Dalton told me that Holly was sleeping with Jada's boyfriend Rodney."

"First of all why would Holly sleep with Rodney? He was such a nerd. And second of all, how did Dalton know about Rodney and Holly?" Jenna asked.

"He spent most of his time following Holly around. I should probably talk to him again at some point. The fact that he was stalking Holly could prove to be useful in figuring out who might have killed her."

"Assuming Dalton isn't the killer himself," Dennis said.

"Yeah, assuming that," Tj agreed.

"Has anyone talked to Rodney?" Dennis wondered. "If he was sleeping with Holly and things went south or if Holly threatened to tell Jada, he could have had a reason to want her dead."

"I don't remember him being at the party on the night that Holly died," Tj said.

Dennis shrugged. "Just because he wasn't at the party doesn't mean he didn't kill her. We still don't have any idea what happened. If you think about it anyone could have done it."

"Great." Tj groaned. "That certainly narrows things down."

"If solving Holly's murder had been easy, it would have been accomplished ten years ago," Dennis pointed out. "Maybe we should focus on who sent Samantha Colton's car over the side of the cliff."

"Did you find out anything new from the autopsy report?" Tj asked Hunter.

"Maybe. We don't have the full labs back, but we do know she didn't have any drugs or alcohol in her system. We've also eliminated death by natural causes such as heart attack or stroke. Based on her injuries, it seems likely she didn't fall asleep at the wheel. Her injuries indicate she braced herself for impact. My guess is she became disoriented on an unfamiliar road during a downpour."

"Roy told me there's a suspicious dent on the left front fender of her car, but so far they don't know if it's connected to the accident," Tj informed the others. "He said the crime scene guys are looking into it."

"Did they find skid marks at the scene?" Dennis asked.

"Only a single set that belonged to Samantha's car. If another vehicle intentionally rammed into her, the driver might not have applied the brakes."

Dennis frowned. "Maybe. But chances are the car that did the ramming would have skidded out of control on impact unless it was going very slowly."

"Maybe we should just drop this whole thing," Jenna said. "Holly has been dead for ten years. The cops couldn't figure out who killed her back then, so there's little chance we can do it all these years later. And if there's even a remote possibility that Samantha Colton wasn't murdered and her death really was an accident, do we really want to go digging around and stirring things up?"

"Jenna makes a good point," Dennis said. "When I spoke to Brett earlier, he told me things were already tense between him and Jessie, and now they're downright intolerable."

"They seemed to be getting along okay at the decorating party," Tj said.

"They were probably putting on a united front for the rest of us."

"I agree that dropping it might make for a more enjoyable reunion but I'm having a hard time letting it go at this point," Tj stated. "My gut is telling me that Samantha's accident wasn't an accident. Besides, now that Samantha has been successful in getting everyone talking about Holly's death I sort of want to figure out what happened."

"I need to call Roy about the autopsy results," Hunter said. "Maybe he'll have news."

"I'll check on the girls while you make your call," Jenna said.

"And I'll get another pitcher of beer," Kyle offered.

Tj was left alone at the table with Dennis.

"You were friends with Nathan in school," Tj said.

"Yeah. We were good friends. Why?"

"Of all the suspects who have been identified, he's the only one who hasn't made an appearance. He didn't come to the school this afternoon, but I know he's staying at Bookman's and has been for several days."

"Nathan was always a loner. Besides, he's famous now and probably busy," Dennis pointed out. "I'm not surprised he didn't want to spend his time hanging streamers."

"Has he called you or made arrangements to get together?"

"No, but I've been working. I'm sure he'll be at the welcome reception tomorrow."

Tj couldn't help but wonder why he'd been part of the top ten on Colton's list. Sure, he'd been seen with Jessie, but Tj didn't understand what that had to do with Holly or her murder.

"Did Nathan ever tell you that I caught him making out with Jessie the day before homecoming?" Tj asked.

Dennis frowned. "Jessie? Really?"

"Saw them with my own two eyes."

"Nathan always told me he loathed girls like Jessie. I

remember him being into Mackenzie, not that she gave any guy the time of day. But Jessie? It doesn't fit."

"I know. Whenever he mentioned the cheerleaders in any of his newspaper articles, he tended to put us down."

"Are you sure you saw what you think you did?" Dennis asked.

"Total lip lock."

"Who's locking lips?" Jenna asked as she returned to the table.

"Nathan and Jessie," Tj answered. She looked up as Hunter came back into the restaurant and headed in their direction, looking down at his phone as he walked. Tj hoped he didn't trip. The fact that she had a bruise on her face was bad enough; if they both ended up with bruises it was going to look like they'd had a boxing match.

"Roy is on his way over," Hunter told them as he sat down. "He said he has news and wanted to tell us all at the same time."

"Let's grab the booth behind us," Jenna said. "We can have the girls sit there when the pizza arrives. Hopefully, Roy won't have anything too gruesome to share. I'm starving, and I don't want my appetite ruined by tales of blood and guts."

"That'd make a fun Halloween special," Tj said.

Jenna frowned at her.

"It'd be easy. The pizza sauce could be the blood and the toppings could be the guts. Sausage comes immediately to mind, but I bet there are other gut-worthy toppings."

"You're a strange woman," Jenna commented.

By the time Roy showed up, the pizza had already arrived. Tj offered him a slice. They each ate their fill, the girls returned to the video arcade, and Roy shared his news.

"Samantha Colton was Holly Riverton's half-sister," Roy announced. "Apparently, Holly's father had an affair with a black woman when Holly was just a baby. The letter asking *Second Look* to investigate Holly's death was a fake. Ms. Colton wrote it herself, and when the program's producers went in a different direction, she decided to investigate on her own."

"But why now? It's been ten years," Jenna said.

"Ms. Colton didn't know about Holly until after their father passed away six months ago. According to her roommate, she became obsessed with finding Holly's killer after she found out about their connection. I imagine she came here this week because the reunion provided an opportunity to interview everyone," Roy said. "I don't know if Ms. Colton was murdered or if her accident really was an accident, but I do think she gave a whole lot of people reasons to want her out of the way during her short time here."

Hunter's phone rang, and he said he needed to take it. He got up from the table and stepped outside while the others continued the conversation.

"Timing indicates Ms. Colton made a phone call shortly before she headed out to Old Sawmill Road," Roy said.

"Maybe she was going to meet whoever she called," Tj proposed.

"That's my theory."

"Do we know who she called?"

"The number was blocked but I have the guys at the crime lab working on it."

"There aren't that many houses out that there. Maybe we can figure out who lives out that way and track the person who made the phone call by the process of elimination," Tj suggested.

"First of all, we don't know that the person she called lives out there. Second there are more houses than it might seem, and third, a lot of people use Old Sawmill road as a shortcut out to the highway, although it certainly isn't a shortcut during a storm. Still if Ms. Colton has one of those travel apps that help you find the most efficient route it could have sent her in that direction."

"So we're back to square one," Tj surmised.

"Maybe. I've got a few ideas, things to look into. Maybe something will pop up if we keep looking. In the meantime, as always, be careful." Roy looked directly at Tj. "And no heroics. If someone intentionally ran Ms. Colton off the road I want them found and brought to justice but not at the risk of injury to my friends."

"We'll be careful," Tj promised. "By the way, any luck unsealing Rebecca Heins interview?"

"Not yet but I'm working on it."

CHAPTER 12

Thursday, October 29

"Does anyone have any questions before we begin?" Tj asked the group of girls who had volunteered to help her with her project.

"Are we actually going to get wet?" one of them asked.

"I think we need to get wet; otherwise it will look phony," another girl replied.

"But my hair is going to frizz," the first girl countered.

"I brought my hairdryer," Tj informed them.

"It's really nice of all of you to do this for me," Lexi said.

"You're our friend," a third girl said. "We're happy to help."

Tj had enlisted twenty girls, many of them from the *it* crowd, to join Lexi in a remake of the video of her singing in the shower. The G-rated video had the girls dressed in shorts and tube tops, but the off-key vocals in the second video was just embarrassing enough to prove a point.

"Okay. Let's do this," Tj said.

When it was finished, Tj uploaded the video to all the popular social media sites with the hashtag showerokee. It took only a few hours for the hysterically funny video to circulate throughout the school, and by the end of the day #showerokee was the new thing, and the majority of the student body was laughing with Lexi rather than at her.

"The video we made this morning was awesome," Carly said to Tj later that afternoon.

"I'm glad you decided to join us," Tj answered.

"I wasn't going to but I spoke to the counselor you set me up with this morning before school. He convinced me that it would be a good idea to participate along with the other girls. I'm glad I did. At first I only went along with your plan because I really want to be on the soccer team, but after just one conversation with the man, I actually think talking to him might help."

Tj hugged Carly. "I'm so happy to hear that. The team wouldn't be the same without you."

"I know my behavior has been a little difficult to deal with. I was just so mad. I still am. But I'm going to do everything I have to in order to be reinstated to the team, and once I am back on the team, I'm going to do everything I can to control my temper."

It always made Tj feel so good when she knew that she'd made a difference in one of her student's lives. Of course there were other students who seemed to be beyond redemption.

"Your video was dumb," Portia said later that day after Tj had called her into her office. "I can't believe Principal Remington let you make it."

"Principal Remington agreed it was a good idea to demonstrate that Lexi's friends had her back. Seems Lexi is more popular than ever."

"That's because people are sheep. They follow whoever has the mic at the moment."

"I noticed that you didn't support the idea to help Lexi," Tj commented.

"So?"

"The fact that you turned me down, along with a few things I've overheard today, suggests to me that you're the one who made and uploaded the video of Lexi in the first place."

"You can't prove that," Portia challenged.

"You're right; I can't prove who did it. What I don't understand is why anyone would do such a thing. It was obviously an attempt to humiliate Lexi. I thought you and she were friends."

"First of all, Lexi and I are no longer friends. Second— and I'm not saying I was the one who did it—but if it *was* me, I would have posted that ridiculous scene to get even with Lexi for spreading rumors."

"What kind of rumors?"

"Why don't you ask her?"

"I could do that but I think it might be better if you just tell me."

"Lexi has been going around telling everyone that I blackballed Carly from the group after Kenny died because I blamed her for his death."

"And did you blackball Carly?"

"Not for the reason she thinks. I don't think it is her fault that Kenny is dead but I do think it is her fault that she has been making everyone's lives so miserable. All she does is whine and complain. Like she is the only one grieving. I'm grieving too. Kenny and I dated off and on for almost a month."

"I'm sure you have been grieving and I understand that grief can make you do things you wouldn't otherwise do, but the fact that Lexi has been sticking up for Carly is no excuse for the video you posted. Bullying in any context is not going to be tolerated by me or the administration of this school. If I find out that you've been bullying Lexi or anyone else, you can be sure I'll be taking the matter up with both Principal Remington and your parents."

Portia laughed. "Go ahead. Catching Lexi in a compromising situation and posting it was my mother's idea in the first place. You should be glad it was me and not Mom who shot the video. Mom wouldn't have been so careful about maintaining a PG rating."

Tj frowned. She didn't know Portia's mother, though she had seen her around campus a time or two. She was what Tj thought of as plastic. It was evident she had had a *lot* of work done to create an image that was about as perfect as fake could be. Tj didn't understand why anyone would submit herself to that much elective surgery, but she supposed you couldn't really understand why anyone did anything unless you had the opportunity to walk in their shoes.

"You realize you just admitted to making the video," Tj pointed out.

Portia stood up. "I did no such thing, and if you say I did,

I'll deny it." She turned to the door. "Trust me, you don't want to get on my mother's bad side. She isn't nearly as nice as I am. If she thinks you're standing in the way of what she wants, she'll chew you up and spit you out."

"And what exactly is it that your mother wants?" Tj asked.

"She wants me to be part of the popular crowd. You may not realize it looking at her now, but my mom was a nobody in high school. She told me she felt invisible the entire four years she went to this school."

"She went here?"

Portia nodded.

"When?"

"Geez, look it up." With that, Portia was gone.

Tj watched her walk away. So Portia's mother had been a wallflower. That could explain a lot. Tj did just what Portia suggested: looked up her mother. A quick search of the girl's school records gave Tj a maiden name, and a search of the alumni database gave her a graduating class. Tj headed over to the library to look Eve Smith up in her yearbook.

"Morning, Betty," Tj greeted the school librarian. "Where can I find the old yearbooks?"

"Back wall, near the emergency exit."

Tj headed to the shelf Betty had indicated and found the correct year. She looked up Eve, but the girl in the photo in no way resembled the woman Tj knew as Portia's mother, who was blond with a small nose, perfectly straight teeth, and large breasts. The girl in the photo had mousy brown hair, a large nose, and crooked teeth. She wore glasses that partially hid her eyes, but Tj could see they were the same deep blue they were today.

"Did you find what you were looking for?" Betty wandered over while Tj was still looking at the photo.

"You've been here a long time. Do you remember this girl?"

Betty looked at the yearbook. "A lot of kids come through here and I don't remember them all, but yeah, I remember her. She was a timid little thing. The other girls tended to pick on her, so she'd come into the library during lunch to do her homework."

"This is Portia Waldron's mother."

Betty frowned. "You're kidding. That blond Barbie doll who struts around here is the same girl who was so skittish in high school she couldn't even talk to the other students?"

"She's obviously had a lot of plastic surgery."

"And a personality transplant," Betty observed.

Tj studied the photo. Things were beginning to make sense in a sick, twisted way.

"Do you remember if this girl was one of the ones who picked on Eve?" Tj pointed to a photo of Chantel.

"I remember Chantel. I'm not sure this school has ever had a bigger queen bee. She used to torture poor Eve."

Tj looked at Betty. "It seems Eve is enacting her revenge by encouraging her daughter to bully the daughter of the girl who made her life hell in high school."

"Portia uploaded that shower video?" Betty asked.

"I believe so. She mentioned it was her mother's idea. At the time, that comment made no sense, but now, sadly, it does. The question is, how do I deal with bullying on campus when the real problem is the bully's mother?"

"Let me get this straight," Greg Remington said when Tj met with him during her afternoon prep. "Portia Waldron all but confessed to being responsible for the video that created such a ruckus, but you think her mother is the one who is actually responsible?"

Tj spelled out exactly what had occurred.

"That's crazy."

"Yes," Tj agreed. "It is."

"How do you suggest we handle this?"

"I don't know if Chantel Michaels realizes Portia's mom is one of the girls she bullied. My guess is she doesn't. Maybe if I explain things she'll be willing to reach out to Eve. If that doesn't work, I think you need to have a conversation with Portia."

Principal Remington sat back in his chair. "I'll speak to Sheila about the situation. Maybe she can help us navigate these murky waters."

"Perfect. And as long as I'm here, I want to ask if it would be okay if Gina covers my class next period so I can go next door to watch the spelling bee. Gracie is a finalist at the school level and Gina has a prep."

"Fine by me. Tell Gracie I wish her luck."

The elementary school had been having spell-offs for weeks to weed the student body down to five students from grades one through three and five from grades four through six, with the winner of each group going on to the regional spelling bee in Carson City. Tj knew the students left standing at this point were all serious competitors who had been studying for months. She really hoped Gracie won. Tj had caught her with a flashlight under the covers going over her word list on more than one occasion.

When Tj entered the school's multipurpose room, she wasn't expecting to see such a massive crowd. Tj hoped Gracie wouldn't be nervous with so many people watching. Tj waved to Hunter, who was sitting on the bleachers near her dad, her grandpa, and Kyle. She made her way across the crowded floor and sat down between Kyle and Hunter.

"I thought you had to work today," Tj greeted Hunter.

"I did. I mean, I do. I couldn't miss seeing our girl compete, so I took a break. I'll need to go back after."

Tj liked the way Hunter said *our girl*. After Tj had been given guardianship of her two sisters, it had occurred to her that her new family status might impede her ability to find a husband and have children of her own. Not a lot of the men she'd dated in the past would have been willing to take on a ready-made family.

"I stopped by to talk to Gracie for a few minutes," Kyle informed her. "She didn't seem nervous at all. She said she'd been studying and she knew all the words."

"She does know all the words," Tj confirmed. "At least all the words they gave her to study. I think if they go through those words and still have more than one contestant in a particular age group, they randomly begin picking other words to break the tie."

The five students left in Gracie's group also included Gracie's friend Loren, who Tj was confident Gracie could outspell; a new student to the school named Brian; an advanced student named Julie, who often beat the other kids in academic competitions; and Trisha, the girl whose parents made her randomly spell words from the dictionary.

"I'm really nervous, even if Gracie isn't," Tj said.

"Yeah, me too," her grandpa admitted. "She's worked so hard for this."

"I think these competitions are harder on the families than on the kids," Mike added.

"Here they come," Tj said.

Everyone clapped as the ten students participating in the spell-off filed into the room. Gracie waved to them as she made her way to the metal folding chairs set out for the contestants. The group from the younger grades would go first.

Tj held her breath through the first few rounds. No one was eliminated. Brian, the only boy in Gracie's group, was the first to miss a word and be eliminated in the eighth round. Tj's heart pounded as the contest continued. Gracie was smiling and seemed to be having fun, but Tj was a wreck watching her.

"Why are your eyes closed?" Hunter whispered to her.

"I can't watch," Tj confessed. They were into the eleventh round and the words were getting harder.

"Do you think it will make a difference to the outcome?"

"Maybe."

Tj listened as Gracie easily spelled her word correctly. By round thirteen Loren had been eliminated.

During round fifteen Trisha stumbled on a word. It broke Tj's heart when she glanced at her parents, who were looking at her with stern expressions on their faces. The poor girl looked like she was going to cry. Gracie reached out and took the girl's hand, which seemed to help, because she managed to spell the word correctly just as time ran out. Trisha received a demerit for the false start but wasn't eliminated; the black mark would only come into play if there was a tie.

Julie was eliminated in the nineteenth round, so it was down to Gracie and Trisha. Tj really wished both girls could win. Her little sister had been working hard and deserved to win, but Trisha looked like her whole world revolved around this one competition.

The old-fashioned clock on the wall ticked down the minutes as the girls continued to correctly spell every word given to them.

When they got to round thirty the announcer informed the crowd that he was about to provide the final word. If both girls got their word correct, Gracie would win because Trisha had the demerit. If Trisha got her word wrong, Gracie was the automatic winner. If Trisha got her word right and Gracie was wrong, Trisha would win.

Trisha's word was achievement, which she spelled correctly.

Tj held her breath as Gracie was given her word.

"Glamour," the announcer said.

Tj smiled. Gracie had struggled with the word, so they'd practiced it until she could spell it in her sleep.

Tj watched as Gracie glanced at Trisha, who had tears running down her face. Then she looked out into the crowd and grinned at Tj.

"Glamour," Gracie said. "G-l-a-m-o-r. Glamour."

"I'm sorry, but that is incorrect," the announcer said. "Trisha is the winner."

"How could she miss glamour?" Ben said. "We practiced that word a hundred times."

Tj looked toward the front of the room. Gracie was

smiling as Trisha's parents hugged and congratulated their successful daughter.

"I think she missed the word on purpose," Tj said.

"Why would she do that?"

"Trisha needed it more."

"That's one special kid we've got ourselves," Mike commented.

"Yes." Tj waved at Gracie, who was waving at her with a huge smile on her face. "We really do."

CHAPTER 13

Later that evening, Tj was tucking the girls into bed before she and Hunter headed out to join Jenna and Dennis at the welcome reception which was being held in the Lakeside Bar and Grill.

"Do we have to go to bed?" Gracie asked.

"Pumpkin looks tired. She's still a baby and babies need a lot of sleep."

"Okay." Gracie scooted down so she was under her covers. Crissy curled up on Gracie's pillow and Pumpkin snuggled up next to them.

"I'm very proud of what you did for Trisha at the spelling bee today."

Gracie shrugged. "I wanted to go to Carson City, but I didn't want Trisha to be sad, and when she almost missed that first word I could see her parents were mad. I knew you wouldn't be mad if I didn't win."

Tj hugged Gracie. "Of course I wouldn't be mad if you didn't win. I'm so proud of how hard you studied, and I'm even prouder of the fact that you were willing to sacrifice to help out your friend. How about if I take you and Ashley to

Carson City in a couple of weeks? We can have lunch and go to the Children's Museum."

"That would be fun. Can Aunt Jenna, Kristi, and Kari come?"

"Absolutely."

"And Dr. Hunter?"

"I will definitely ask him."

"And Uncle Kyle?"

"We can invite anyone you want."

"I'm glad we have a big family."

"Me too, pumpkin, me too."

Tj tucked the covers around Gracie and kissed her on the forehead.

"How come you're going to sleep in a cabin instead of your room?" Gracie asked as Tj began to straighten up.

"Because a lot of my friends are staying in cabins, and I thought it would be fun to sleep in one like everyone else."

"Are you taking Echo?"

"No, he's staying here."

"Can he sleep with me and Pumpkin?"

"Actually," Tj said, "that's a really good idea."

Tj called Echo into the room and had him lie on the floor next to Gracie's bed. She knew her sister felt better having him there, and Echo wouldn't want to sleep in her room alone. Tj kissed Gracie once again and then turned off the light. "Love you to the moon and back."

"Love you even farther." Gracie yawned.

When Gracie was all tucked in, Tj headed to Ashley's room. This sister wasn't one to welcome physical displays of affection these days, but no matter what else was going on she still liked to be tucked in at night.

"Can Kristi spend the night tomorrow?" Ashley asked as Tj tucked the covers in around her burrito style.

"I think it might be best if everyone stayed at their own house tomorrow while the adults are busy with the reunion. Maybe Kristi and Kari can stay over Saturday night after you get back from Aspen's party. We can have a Halloween slumber party. I'll talk to Jenna about it."

"I thought you were going to sleep in one of the cabins this weekend."

"Yeah, that was the plan, but the more I think about it, the more I realize I want to spend Halloween night with you and Gracie."

"Can we sleep in sleeping bags in the den and watch movies all night?"

Tj could remember doing just that when she was a kid. She and her friends would compete to see who could stay awake the longest. No one ever made it all the way until morning, but it was fun to try.

"We'll see."

"We'll see means no."

"We'll see means we'll see," Tj countered.

Tj kissed Ashley on the forehead as Midnight curled up on the pillow next to Ashley's head. "Sweet dreams and don't let the bedbugs bite."

"Do you think I'm pretty?" Ashley said just as Tj was about to close the door.

"I think you're absolutely stunning."

"Really? You aren't just saying that because you're my sister?"

Tj walked back into the room and sat down on the side of Ashley's bed. "Really. Why do you ask?" She'd been dealing with bullying all week. She certainly hoped Ashley hadn't fallen victim to the ruthless pastime girls of all ages seemed to like to participate in.

"One of the girls in my class was making fun of my red hair and freckles. She said red hair was dumb and none of the boys will ever want to go on dates with me as long as I have freckles."

Tj tucked a strand of Ashley's hair behind her ear. "Your red hair is beautiful. When you get older all the other girls are going to be so jealous of it because you'll stand out from the crowd. And as for the freckles, they fade. I had a lot more when I was your age than I did by the time I got into high school."

"Really?"

"Really. And even if they don't fade, you should wear them proudly. They give your face character. They make you unique."

"Adults always say things like that, but I don't want to be unique. I just want to fit in."

Tj could remember feeling exactly like Ashley at her age, with her frizzy auburn hair and freckles.

"I like your freckles, and I bet the boys will as well, but if they don't fade and you still don't like them by the time you're in high school I can help you pick out a lightweight concealer."

"You mean like makeup?"

"Yeah. Like makeup."

Ashley smiled. "Okay."

Tj kissed her again and once again headed for the door. There were times when Tj wondered how her life would have turned out if Ashley and Gracie hadn't come to live with her.

It would certainly be different and, Tj suspected, it would certainly be a lot easier. But that easy was empty, and she knew in her heart she wouldn't give up what she had for all the easy in the world.

Tj went to her bedroom to pack an overnight bag. She supposed it was silly to go to all the trouble to reserve a cabin for the next few nights, but she knew both she and Hunter desperately needed some couple time. The girls would be fine with her dad and grandpa, and Hunter had asked one of Jake's old friends from out of the area if he'd like to come for a visit this weekend. Jake probably realized the timing of his friend's trip was a huge coincidence, but he really did need to have someone nearby and Hunter really did need some time away.

"Alone at last." Hunter pulled Tj into his arms the minute she walked through the door of the cabin where he was waiting for her.

"We're already late for the welcome reception," Tj reminded him. "And as much as I'd love to skip the reception and stay here with you, there are some people that I really want to talk to."

Hunter sighed. "I imagine everyone who is still on your suspect list should be here tonight. Maybe we can get this mystery wrapped up and enjoy the rest of our weekend?"

Tj kissed Hunter. "I really do hope so. I know we've really been looking for some alone time together, and I know it's tough to find alone time when we both live with family members. But now that I'm involved in this investigation, I need to see it through."

"I know. The fact that you care so much about others is part of the reason I love you. How can I help?"

"I don't really have a plan at this point other than to go to the reception and talk to people and see where that leads us."

"Did you ever get ahold of either Jada or Mia?" Hunter asked.

"No I called and left messages for both but haven't heard back so far. Mia's personal assistant said something about her being out of town. I got the impression she wasn't even going to give her the message until she returned so I'm not holding out a lot of hope that she will get back to me, but the message I left for Jada was on her personal cell so maybe she'll actually receive it and call me back."

"I sincerely doubt either is guilty of any wrongdoing, but I suppose it couldn't hurt to see what, if anything, they remember."

"If I don't hear from Jada this evening I'll call her back tomorrow. I know she has a really busy life with a lot of responsibility and although all of us here at the party are in long weekend mode it is Thursday and Jada is probably simply in work mode."

"To be honest I'm having a hard time mentally transitioning from work mode to party mode after the week I've had but I plan to try." Hunter laced his fingers through Tj's. "Should we go?"

"I'm ready."

The Lakeside Bar and Grill was packed when they walked in. It looked like everyone was having a good time. "It looks like pretty much everyone showed," Tj commented.

"It's a good turnout," Hunter agreed as he looked around

the room. "There are people here I haven't seen since high school."

"Oh look. It's Mr. Bartholomew." Tj pointed toward a balding man in his late fifties who taught history when they were in school.

"I know the reunion committee invited several of the teacher's involved with the senior class back then. I'm pretty sure there are several who have agreed to attend. I ran into Mrs. Valdez at the post office the other day and she said she planned to be here."

Mrs. Valdez taught English ten years ago but had since retired.

"Is that Coach Fremont at the bar?" Tj asked as she scanned the room.

Hunter nodded. "It is. Boy it's been awhile. I heard he moved to Carson City after he retired."

"I thought he moved to Kansas after he left Serenity High."

"He did but he moved back to the area a couple of years ago. Do you want to go over and say hi?"

"He's talking to Brett now. Maybe later."

The truth was, Tj didn't want to talk to the coach at all. Bob Fremont had been the football coach when Hunter and Tj were in high school. Hunter had really liked Fremont, but Tj never shared his enthusiasm for the man. Sure, he was a man's man who got the most out of his boys and created a winning team year after year, but he was also a lady's man who tended to look at high school girls in a way teachers never should. She'd shared her discomfort with Hunter when they were in high school. He'd tried to convince her she was just imagining the inappropriate looks the coach was sending in her direction but Tj knew that imagination hadn't played any part in her feeling of revulsion for the man.

"Do you want a drink?" Hunter asked.

"Maybe a glass of wine. I think I'll just wait here, if you don't mind getting it for me."

"Something wrong?"

Tj shrugged. "I just need a minute before heading into the fray."

Tj watched Hunter walk away. She wandered off to the side and stared out the window. It had been an emotionally draining week, and seeing Coach Fremont again had brought back a series of jumbled, bad memories from her senior year. It was almost like she knew something her conscious mind wasn't yet willing to deal with.

As far as Tj knew, Coach Fremont had never actually gone so far as to act on his flirting with high school girls, but his obvious glances had been enough to make her feel like he'd actually touched her. Tj understood why the guys never saw it. Fremont saved his long, meaningful stares for those times he happened to catch a girl alone. Tj knew there were several cheerleaders who'd complained among themselves about the unwanted attention, but no one had been willing to bring their concerns to the adults in their lives.

"Wine for my lady," a voice said from behind her. Tj turned around and accepted the glass from Kyle.

"What are you doing here?" Tj asked.

"Hunter was waylaid by that obnoxious coach and asked me to bring you your drink."

"No, I mean, what are you doing here in the bar at this party? Not that you aren't welcome. I'm actually really glad to see you."

"See the blonde in the red dress?" Kyle nodded toward the bar.

"Connie?"

"She invited me to be her date for the evening. At first I wasn't going to accept, but then I realized I didn't want to stay home by myself. I doubt she'll even remember I was here in the morning. She's smashed."

"How did you meet her?"

"I came by to drop off Pumpkin's leash and chew toy, which we'd left at my house. I was chatting with your grandpa when I heard something in the bushes. It was Connie."

"What was Connie doing in the bushes?" Tj shook her head and held up her hand. "Never mind, I don't want to know. Are you sure you want to spend the whole evening with someone bound to puke on your shoes?"

"I'm not going to stay the whole evening. I just wanted to say hi to everyone and meet your friends."

"Come to the game with us tomorrow. My dad is going to call to ask you to go with him, but you should come with Hunter, Jenna, Dennis, and me."

"Thanks, but I don't want to be a third wheel—or, in this case, a fifth wheel. I'd love to go with your dad and the girls, though, so I'll call him to arrange it."

"He's awake. You can stop by the house."

Kyle looked at Connie hanging all over the guy standing next to her.

"Maybe I'll just go now," Kyle said. "Before your dad heads to bed and before Connie actually does puke on my shoes."

"Good idea."

Kyle kissed Tj on the cheek and headed out the side door. Tj watched him walk away and then returned her attention to the bar, where Coach Fremont was talking much too loud to be considered appropriate. Tj frowned. There was a memory just out of reach. She really hated that feeling, when you knew you knew something but couldn't remember what it was.

"Penny for your thoughts," Hunter said in her ear as he wrapped his arms around her from behind.

"No thoughts. Just taking a minute to enjoy the wine Kyle brought me."

Hunter kissed her neck. "I know you well enough to realize when you're feeling unsettled. Is it the investigation?"

Tj shrugged but didn't say anything.

Hunter kissed her shoulder. "Is it Coach Fremont? I know you never really liked him."

"You're right, I've never been a fan of Coach Fremont, but I suspect my slightly melancholy mood has more to do with the investigation," Tj was afraid a discussion about Coach Fremont would lead to an argument, just like it often had in high school. Tj turned around and put her arms around Hunter's neck, then looked him in the eye. "In the past ten years, have you given any thought to what really happened to Holly?"

"Honestly? No. We were kids when she died. There was no reason not to leave the investigation to the cops. Holly's family moved while we were away at college, and when we returned we were busy establishing our careers and starting our lives."

"Yeah, I guess, but it's odd that I wasn't more curious."

"It wasn't our job to wonder," he assured her.

"Maybe. But now that Samantha Colton is dead, chances are the Sheriff's Department will let the whole thing fade onto a very distant back burner again. I never once thought about Holly's death after those first few shocking weeks, but now I find it hard to think about anything else."

Hunter rested his chin on the top of her head. "I have to admit I agree. Colton did unearth some interesting facts before her accident. She died while trying to find out the truth. I guess it would be a shame if no one followed up on what she started."

"So what do we do?"

Hunter pulled back and looked Tj in the eye. "Samantha Colton was getting somewhere because she wasn't afraid to ask the hard questions. She didn't know these people; we do. Are you ready to do that with the people in this room? Our friendships might not survive it."

"The people in this room mean a lot to me. We share a history. I'd hate to start digging around and risk those relationships, but at this point I need to see it through. I say we quietly investigate while trying not to ruffle too many feathers."

"Okay so where do we start?"

Tj looked around the room. Most of the people on Colton's list were at the party. "Colton listed Brett as her number-one suspect. We know she spoke to him the night of the accident. Jessie verified that Brett was upset about the questions she was asking, but when we saw him on Wednesday he seemed happy and relaxed. Roy hadn't made public the fact that Colton was dead until today. If Brett already knew that Colton was dead, that would've explained his good mood. In addition, we know the place where Holly was last seen alive was a party held at Brett's house, and that he was responsible for inviting most of the people who showed up. We also know Brett didn't particularly care for Holly due to her relationship with Jessie. I think his rank as number one suspect in both cases is warranted. If Brett killed Holly, he would have had to leave the house at some point," Tj realized. "Chances are Jessie was staying over, so we just need to ask Jessie if Brett was with her the entire evening."

"Unless Jessie killed Holly," Hunter added.

"Okay, so I'll strike up a conversation with Jessie and see if I can slip the question into the conversation, and you talk to Brett, and we'll compare notes afterward," Tj suggested.

"Sounds good to me."

Tj headed toward where Jessie was standing talking to a girl whose name Tj couldn't remember. Her first task was going to be to get Jessie alone.

"Hey Jessie. Are you having a good time?" Tj asked.

"I am. You remember Sally?"

Tj frowned. "I'm sorry I don't.'

"Don't worry about it," Sally laughed. "I didn't transfer in until my senior year. A lot of people here tonight don't remember me."

"Well I'm glad you came." Tj offered a smile.

"Me too. I wasn't going to until I heard there was an open bar." Sally glanced down at her empty glass. "Which reminds me, that I was heading for a refill when I ran into Jessie."

"Good talking to you," Jessie said as Sally walked away.

"I feel bad I didn't recognize her," Tj said after Sally left.

"Don't worry I didn't recognize her either," Jessie laughed. "She seemed to know me so I played along. I'm afraid I've had to do that several times tonight. Some people look exactly the same as they did in high school, and others look so different."

"As long as I have you alone can I talk to you for a minute?" Tj asked.

"Is it about Holly?"

"Yes.'

Jessie sighed. "I figured as much. A few people have mentioned that you've been looking into things on the side. As much as I hate to ruin the party with thoughts of that night, I guess I wouldn't be the person I strive to be if I didn't help you out." Jessie looked around the room. "But let's go outside. It's getting stuffy in here."

Tj led Jessie out onto the deck. There was an almost full moon glistening on the lake creating a cozy and romantic atmosphere. It was a cool evening but there were fires in the pits and portable heaters set around the perimeter of the seating area. Tj and Jessie found a bench near one of the fire pits away from the others who were enjoying the night air.

"I really don't know what happened," Jessie informed her after Tj broached the subject. "Holly and I got into a fight. We'd been fighting a lot actually so in a way it wasn't even that huge of an occurrence."

"Why had you and Holly been fighting?"

"Holly and I had a long history together. Most of the time I really valued her opinion, but Holly really didn't like Brett and she was putting a lot of pressure on me to break up with him. I loved Holly, but I also loved Brett, so I was having a hard time making up my mind about whether to listen to her or not."

"Why did Holly want you to break up with Brett?"

"For some reason, Brett and Holly got off on the wrong foot. She didn't like him from day one. I tried to get her to see what a good guy he was but she was constantly pointing out things about him that she found fault with. She said she was just trying to make sure I didn't get hurt but Brett thought she was jealous of our relationship and was simply making things up."

"Like what kinds of things?"

"Just things like the fact that he had a wandering eye or he didn't treat me with the respect he should have. Stupid stuff really. I guess if I am honest the allegations that Holly constantly made about Brett were beginning to get to me, and I was so, so, tired of arguing with her. I promised Holly after one of our bigger arguments that I'd break up with Brett after the homecoming dance. I sure as heck wasn't going to do it before the dance and risk not having a date. When we got to Brett's house Holly reminded me of my promise but I was beginning to have second thoughts. Deep down I guess I knew that half the stuff Holly used to tell me about Brett were exaggerations. Anyway, after I told Holly that I was reconsidering my promise to break up with Brett, she went crazy. I'd never seen her so mad. She was making a scene so I convinced her to come upstairs with me so we could talk without everyone at the party overhearing our conversation."

"And after you got upstairs?"

"We argued for a while, but eventually Holly left. I was tired and emotionally drained, so I climbed into Brett's bed and went to sleep. Brett eventually joined me and we slept in until noon the next day. I never saw Holly again."

Jessie looked grieved by the thought. "Wow that must have been really tragic for you."

"It was. I was a total mess for months. Poor Brett didn't know how to help me and my parents were about at the end of their rope with my depression and bouts of crying. But as odd as this is going to seem, a part of me felt relief. Don't get me wrong, I didn't want Holly to die, but she had become so possessive of me. When I first met her she was fun and carefree. We had a lot of fun together and really became close, but toward the end she seemed to want to control every aspect of my life."

"Holly was alone at the party but she went to the dance with Dusty Baker. Do you know why he didn't come to the party with her?"

"Holly only went to the dance with Dusty because she needed a date. She was the homecoming queen and it wouldn't be right for her to go alone, but she hadn't originally planned to go so she hadn't thought about a date. Holly didn't even like Dusty, but he was cute and popular so she used him."

"So Holly didn't have a boyfriend?"

"No. At least not one that she admitted to. Although, I think she might have had a guy on the side. Someone she kept secret from everyone even me."

Tj hadn't seen that coming. "A secret guy? Why do you say that?"

Jessie frowned. "It's not like she ever said anything about a guy and I never saw her with a guy, but she seemed different toward the end. We'd have plans to hang out and she'd cancel at the last minute. She never would say why she cancelled or where she had gone, if she had indeed gone anywhere. She was really secretive, and one time I went over to her house when we hadn't made specific plans. Her mom let me in so I headed up to her room. When I let myself in she was sitting on her bed writing in a journal. She closed it real quick when she saw me and put it in a trunk she had at the foot of the bed. There was a padlock on the trunk which she made sure to lock. I asked her what she was doing but she just mumbled something about homework. I know I never kept my homework in a locked trunk. Did you?"

"No. And Holly never mentioned anything that would identify this guy, if there even was a guy?"

"No. It was really kind of odd. Although the more I think about it the oddness of her behavior was widespread I just didn't realize it at the time."

"What do you mean by oddness?"

A slight breeze had come up so Jessie scooted closer to the fire. "For one thing there was the whole situation with the homecoming dance. Holly was pretty and popular but sort of a loner. She never cared about things like homecoming and then out of the blue she tells me she is going to run and she is going to win. I was as shocked as everyone else when she announced her intent to run. And then when she actually won? I thought she'd be thrilled but she didn't even seem to care all that much about the dance. I tried to convince her to go with one of the many guys who asked her and actually wanted to go with her, but she decided to strong-arm Dusty into going with her instead."

"Dusty didn't want to go with her?"

"No. He even had another date but I guess she fell down some stairs at the last minute and broke her leg so she wasn't able to attend the dance. Of course the minute the crowning ceremony was over Holly left both the dance and her date firmly in the dust. It was really very odd."

Odd seemed like an understatement.

"So she left the dance and came to the party with you. Did she talk to anyone or seem to spend time with anyone specifically once she got to the party?"

"Other than me no."

"Do you remember anything at all from that night that could help narrow down who Holly's killer might be? Someone acting odd or maybe someone out of place?"

"Honestly, I was drunk and totally absorbed with how I was going to handle the situation with Brett. I can't even remember who all was at the party. I really do hope you figure out who did this. Holly wasn't the sweet person she pretended to be but she didn't deserve to die."

"You mentioned before that there were at least a half dozen people better off with Holly dead. What did you mean by that?"

"Holly was blackmailing people. I don't want to point fingers at anyone since I really don't know what Holly had on these individuals, but you might want to talk to both Jada and Mackenzie."

"Okay, I will. And thanks for talking to me."

"I guess I'll head in and see if I can salvage what is left of this reunion."

"Okay, have a good night."

After Tj finished talking to Jessie she went in search of Hunter. It would be interesting to see if Brett's story matched up with Jessie's.

"Brett said Jessie was in 'one of her moods' the night of the party," Hunter jumped right in before Tj had a chance to share. "They got into a fight and Jessie and Holly went upstairs. He stayed downstairs and partied with the rest of us until the early hours of the morning. When he went upstairs, Jessie was in his bed and Holly was gone. He crawled in bed with her and they slept until noon the next day."

"Jessie said something similar, only she said it was Holly and she who argued, not she and Brett. She told me she'd promised Holly she'd break up with Brett after homecoming, but at the party she started having second thoughts. When she told Holly as much, Holly went berserk. Jessie claimed she took Holly upstairs so they could talk without everyone overhearing. They argued for a while, and Holly got mad and left. Jessie climbed into Brett's bed, went to sleep, and never saw Holly again."

"So unless they are both lying it looks like neither of them did it."

"Jessie didn't seem like she was lying although Brett's parents' house had that back staircase. It's possible Jessie could have followed Holly outside when she left, killed her, and then returned and crawled into bed."

"And it's possible Brett could have seen Holly leave, followed and killed her, and then returned to the party."

Tj sighed. "In other words we haven't eliminated anyone, although Jessie suggested I speak to both Jada and Mackenzie."

"Jada isn't here and we already talked about the fact that she hadn't called you back, but Mackenzie is." Hunter pointed out. "I can strike up a conversation with her if you'd like."

"I'll talk to her. Why don't you try to talk to Dalton? The fact that Dalton was basically stalking Holly makes me think he might know more than even he thinks he knows. Maybe we can stimulate a memory."

"Okay. He's with a large group at the bar and he's had a few drinks but I'll try."

"Did you happen to see Teddy this evening?" Tj asked Hunter.

"No. Why?"

"He said he'd bring some photos that had been taken at the party. I'll have to track him down tomorrow if he doesn't show."

"I'll keep an eye out for him."

Tj headed into the throng to look for Mackenzie. It looked like everyone including Jenna and Dennis were having a good time. Jenna and Dennis had been through a few rough patches as of late and she was happy to see that they seemed to be relaxed and smiling. She was about to stop by and say hi when her phone buzzed. It was Roy.

"Hey Roy. What's up?" Tj greeted as she retreated to the hallway where there weren't so many people standing around.

"I managed to obtain the witness report Rebecca Heins provided to the sheriff's office ten years ago."

"And."

"Rebecca saw Holly push Lori Jeffries down a flight of stairs."

"Let me guess. She broke her leg and was unable to attend the homecoming dance with her date, Dusty Baker."

"How'd you know?"

"I've been working the case too," Tj reminded him. "Did the deputies at the time suspect either Lori or Dusty of killing Holly?"

Tj could hear Roy rustling the paperwork she imagined he held. "Lori was still in the hospital following surgery on her leg when Holly was killed, but they did question Dusty. It seems that Dusty did not want to take Holly to the dance, but she knew he'd been doing steroids and she threatened to out him if he didn't take her. He told her he already had a date, and the next thing he knew his date was in the hospital."

"Sounds like he had a motive."

"It does, but he had an alibi. When Holly left the dance, he went to the hospital to visit Lori. After he left the hospital, he went home. At the time of the original interview ten years ago, his parents were around to verify this. I guess they were killed in a car accident a few years later."

"And Dusty. Where is he now?"

"Dallas, Texas."

"So unless his parents lied to protect him it doesn't sound like Dusty is our guy. I did get a new lead. Jessie said that she thought that Holly had a secret guy on the side. Someone even she didn't know the identity of."

"Interesting."

"Yeah, it is but I don't know what we can do with that information now. If Holly was the only one to know the identity of her mystery guy, provided she actually had one and Jessie wasn't just imagining things, her secret died with her.

"So it would seem. I'll let you get back to your party. I knew you were trying to get ahold of Rebecca and didn't want you to waste your time. I'll see you tomorrow."

"Okay. Goodnight."

After Tj hung up she went back into the restaurant and looked for Mackenzie. She saw her standing near the bar.

"Nice party," Mackenzie complimented Tj when she joined her.

"Thank you. I think it turned out well."

"I can see that the reunion committee has worked hard on the entire weekend. Too bad the whole thing has been marred by Ms. Colton's investigation, not to mention her death."

"At first I was really upset that the reunion might be ruined with talk of Holly's murder, but I have to admit that there have been some interesting questions that have come from Samantha's investigation."

"I suppose."

"The way Brett's party unfolded was kind of odd if you think about it."

Mackenzie looked toward the ground. "I don't really remember much at all. I only showed up at the party because I was looking for someone who wasn't there. I left after a few minutes."

"Really who were you looking for?"

Mackenzie looked at Tj and shrugged. "Just a guy I was interested in."

"I guess that explains why you were there. I don't remember you hanging around with Holly in high school," Tj commented, watching Mackenzie's face for a reaction to her questions.

"I didn't. We were definitely not in the same social group."

"I do remember someone mentioning that you had some sort of a grudge against her."

"Grudge? I barely knew her. I really can't imagine what this person was talking about. I think I'm going to get another drink. It was nice talking to you."

By the time Tj finished speaking to Mackenzie, Hunter

had wandered out onto the deck so she grabbed a drink from the bar and joined him.

"Any luck?" Hunter asked.

"Mackenzie said she only showed up at the party because she was looking for someone, although she refused to say who. When the individual didn't show up she left. I do remember seeing her leave while we were still there and it did seem that she was only there for a few minutes. She didn't know Holly all that well and I can't imagine what motive she might have had to kill her. She did seem to be hiding something when I spoke to her at the decorating party though."

"Why do you say that?"

"She made a comment about everyone having secrets."

"A lot of people have secrets."

"Do you have secrets?" Tj asked.

Hunter looked surprised by her question. "Why are you asking me that now? You don't think I killed Holly, do you?"

"No, silly. Jenna said she and Dennis confessed all the lies they'd told each other and all the secrets they'd kept before they got married so they could start with a clean slate. Do you think we should do that?"

"Probably not," Hunter said. "Not that I have any big, dark secrets, but we were apart for several years and we both had other relationships during that time. I'm not sure I see the wisdom in opening that can of worms."

"Yeah, you're right," Tj agreed. "Did you find out anything from Dalton?"

"Marianne was glued to his side, so I couldn't really bring up that night. Besides, he's smashed so I doubt I would have gotten anything coherent out of him anyway. I'm glad that Dalton and Marianne decided to rent a cabin for the night even though they live in town. Neither of them are fit to drive."

"I'll try talking to him again tomorrow. As for the other suspects, Mia and Jada aren't here and don't plan to attend, so I don't see how we can confirm or eliminate them as suspects tonight unless someone we do speak to can verify their movements that night. I don't know what's up with Nathan. I know he's in town, but I have yet to actually see him."

"I'm sure he'll be at the game tomorrow; we can talk to him then."

"So is that it?" Tj asked. "Have we done what we can for tonight?"

"I think we have," Hunter confirmed.

"So about that totally empty cabin waiting just down the walkway."

"It would be a shame to let it go to waste."

CHAPTER 14

Friday, October 30

Friday turned out to be the perfect day for football. It was sunny and warm with a light breeze that prevented it from becoming hot even for those sitting on the crowded bleachers. The mountains surrounding the football stadium were painted in fall colors that provided a contrast to the deep blue of the crystal-clear sky. Tj let the enthusiasm of the crowd wash over her as she cheered and chanted for the boys who had come out to give it their all.

Nathan had finally made an appearance, which seemed to provide an added element of excitement for the slightly hungover alumni. He was probably the most famous member of their graduating class next to Mia. He didn't have the overall presence Mia possessed, but he was enough of a celebrity that most of the townsfolk knew who he was and stopped by to say hi.

"Maybe it's a good thing Mia didn't come to the

reunion," Tj said to Jenna sitting to her left. "Nathan has created enough of a stir. There probably would have been a mob begging for autographs if Mia were here."

"Still, I'm sorry she didn't show. We weren't close in high school, but I considered her a friend."

"Maybe we should have tried to convince her to come, although her assistant did say she was out of town so I suppose it is possible that she didn't come for an entirely different reason than her interview with Samantha Colton."

"Maybe." Jenna shrugged. "Something might have come up at the last minute. Mia certainly has a lot more to lose now than when we were in high school, but making choices based on avoidance never seemed to be her style. If you remember, she seemed to thrive on adversity. In fact, it wouldn't be too far off base to say she sought it out. Of course that was ten years ago and people do change, but if I had to wager a bet, I'd say it was a conflict in her schedule rather than a fear of Samantha Colton that caused her to cancel."

"Did you see that outfit she wore to the Academy Awards last year? It seemed like she was intentionally trying to make a fashion *don't* statement, while everyone around her was going for a fashion *do*."

"She certainly is an individual."

While Mia might have cancelled due to a conflict Tj had a feeling the same wasn't true of Jada. She was bright and confident and motivated but she also seemed to be a lot more vulnerable to vicious attacks and gossip by others. Maybe she actually did cheat on her midterms and didn't want to provide a platform for Samantha Colton to share that information. But even if she *had* cheated, it couldn't possibly make a difference now. Jada was a multimillionaire with her own software company. Tj doubted anyone would care what she might have done when she was eighteen.

There was always the possibility that Colton had been correct—Jada had cheated and Holly had blackmailed her into hacking the email accounts of selected students. If that had occurred and Holly had used the access to bully students, could one of them have found out who was responsible and killed her? Jada still hadn't called her back so Tj would try her again as soon as she had the opportunity.

"I'm going to head over to the snack bar before the game starts." Hunter, who was sitting to Tj's left and had been chatting with Brett, interrupted her thoughts. "Anyone want anything?"

"I could use something to eat," Dennis said. "I'll go with you."

"Yeah, I'll come too," Brett seconded. "I have no idea where Jessie went off to."

Tj and Jenna asked for soft drinks, then the guys made their way through the crowd.

"I didn't see much of you and Hunter last night," Jenna commented after they had gone.

"We just wanted some alone time," Tj said as she looked back toward the field. "I like the new uniforms the cheerleaders designed for the game."

The uniforms were cute but skimpy. Tj remembered the cold autumn nights when the squad she had been part of chose to wear their sleeveless tops despite the chill in the air. At least the sun was out today, providing a certain level of warmth without making her too hot in her Serenity High sweatshirt.

"They are cute."

"Sometimes I feel like we just graduated yesterday and other times it's like high school was a million years ago."

"Doreen Sullwold said the same thing when I was talking to her last night," Jenna said. "I got the feeling, though, that she was glad high school was nothing more than a memory."

"Really? Why?"

"She didn't say specifically, but I think it had to do with the fact that she really wasn't very popular."

Tj's phone beeped, indicating she had a text.

"It's Teddy," Tj said. "His wife and one of his kids are sick, so he's not going to make it to the game. He wants to meet in the parking lot and give me those photos I wanted to see."

"It looks like Dennis and the guys are heading this way, so go ahead. I think I can save all the seats until they get here."

Tj stood up. "Hopefully, I can get to the parking lot and back before kickoff."

She jogged down the bleachers and onto the track that ran in front of them, then continued toward the parking lot. She didn't know if the photos would reveal anything significant about Holly's murder, but she wanted to check them out to be sure.

The game was due to start in less than ten minutes, so everyone in attendance was already in the stadium. Tj looked around the mostly deserted parking lot until she saw Teddy's car parked in the very back. Tj waved at him and then headed in his direction.

"Sorry I had to park so far away, but the lot was full when I arrived," Teddy explained.

"No problem. I appreciate your taking the time away

from your sick family to drive the photos over. I'm sorry you're going to miss the game and the dance."

"I'm sorry to miss the game, but I wasn't planning on attending the dance," Teddy informed her. "I didn't like dances when I was in high school, and I think I'd like them even less now."

"I'll text you the highlights during the game," Tj said.

"That'd be nice." Teddy smiled. He handed her an envelope. "I guess I didn't develop all the film I ended up with. I thought I had, but after I pulled everything out I found a roll of undeveloped film in the bottom of the envelope. I don't know if it's still good, but I figured if you really wanted to see what's on it you could try to make prints."

"My friend Kyle has a darkroom in his house. I can have him see what he can recover. Thanks again for bringing everything over."

"No problem. I was actually looking for an excuse to get out of the house for a few minutes. Enjoy the game."

Tj was walking back to the bleachers when she passed Hunter heading out to the parking lot himself.

"Emergency?" Tj guessed.

"One of my patients had a heart attack. His second. I really need to go. I'm sorry. I know this was supposed to be our weekend."

"No problem." Tj stood on tiptoe and gently kissed Hunter on the lips. "Will you make it back in time for the dance?"

"I'll have to assess the situation once I get there. I'll call you and let you know what's going on. Given what I know, I suspect surgery might be our only option."

TJ touched Hunter's arm. "I'm sorry about your patient.

And don't worry about me. I'll be waiting for you when you get done."

Hunter hugged her. "I love you."

"I love you too."

He turned and headed toward his car and Tj continued toward the bleachers. As promised, Jenna had saved her seat, and Jessie had taken the seat Hunter had vacated. Mackenzie was sitting in front of Jessie and Doreen was sitting next to her. Tj didn't want to look at the photos with Jessie sitting right next to her, so she turned around before anyone noticed and headed toward her office. She texted Jenna to let her know she was going to be a few minutes longer.

Tj sat down at her desk and opened the envelope that held both the unprocessed film and the prints from the cameras Teddy had processed. Most of the photos were of people drinking, being silly, and making rude gestures toward the cameraperson. Tj had forgotten how truly out of control a lot of the partygoers had been that night. She cringed when she came across a particularly unflattering photo of herself dancing.

"Yikes." Tj tore the photo in several pieces and tossed it in the trash. That was one image she had no desire to save for nostalgia's sake.

Most of the photos didn't prove or disprove anything. Many were so blurry you could barely make out who was even in them. But Tj felt her breath catch as she looked at images of Holly that had been taken just hours before she was brutally murdered. In most of the photos, she was either standing alone or with Jessie.

Tj continued to thumb through the photos, making a comment out loud about each one as she did so. "Funny,

funny, embarrassing, disgusting, hysterical, what was she thinking, embarrassing, annoying, kill me now, what the heck?"

Tj stared at the photo in her hand. In the background, behind the image of Brett and one of the other guys on the team chugging beer, was an image that was blurry at best but looked an awful lot like Coach Fremont. Tj didn't remember him being at the party. Yes, she'd been slightly tipsy thanks to Brett's spiked punch, but she was certain she would have remembered if the man had been present. What was even odder was that he seemed to be looking at something or someone out of camera range, not at the foolish boys who would both puke before the contest was over.

Tj continued to stare at the photo as she challenged her brain to remember the events of the evening. She quickly thumbed through the rest, but the coach didn't appear in any except the chugging photo. She needed to see the as-yet undeveloped roll of film.

She texted Kyle:

I need a favor. Can you get away and meet me in my office?

Is everything okay?

Yeah, I just need to talk to you. Alone.

On my way.

Tj went back through the photos at a slower pace and examined the people standing around in each one. The teens taking the photos were as wasted as the friends they were taking photos of, so many of the photos were blurry and off center.

There were several more of herself that she decided to destroy before Kyle got to her office. She usually had a good sense of humor about such things, but there were a couple of photos she didn't want *anyone* to see *ever*. The really annoying thing was that every single image of Hunter was drop-dead gorgeous. Of course he was driving and he had always been very responsible, so he hadn't had anything at all to drink, which meant that he wasn't making funny faces or placing himself in embarrassing situations.

"What's up?" Kyle asked as he joined Tj in the office and sat down across from her.

Tj explained about the photos and the unprocessed film.

"Yeah, I can develop it."

"Take a look here." Tj pointed to the blurry background in one of the photos. "What do you think that is?"

"I'm not sure. I can probably clean up the background. You want me to do it now?"

"As much as I want to watch the game," Tj said. "I really want to do this now."

"No problem. I'll go back and tell everyone I'm leaving."

"Don't tell them why. I don't want to bring this to anyone's attention, and you never know who might overhear a random comment."

"Don't worry, I'll make something up. Is your car here?"

"No. I came with Hunter and he got called to the hospital."

"I'll meet you at my car then."

Tj called Jenna rather than returning to her own seat. She hadn't left anything behind, so she didn't have a reason to go back, and she didn't want to face everyone yet. She'd never been a convincing liar.

"Hey, Tj, where are you?" Jenna asked when she picked up.

"Just listen to what I say and don't say anything other than what I tell you to say."

Jenna remained silent.

"Say 'oh, that's too bad.'"

"Oh, that's too bad," Jenna said.

"I found something in the photos Teddy brought me that might be relevant. I really want to check it out and Kyle has agreed to help me. We're heading to his house now, so I won't be back. I think it's best if you stay to watch the game. I don't want to tip anyone off, and if you and Dennis suddenly leave, it might seem suspicious. Everyone knows Hunter got called away, so I want you to tell them that I partied too hard last night and have a massive headache. Tell them Hunter is going to drop me back at the resort to take a nap before the dance tonight. Say 'I understand.'"

"I understand," Jenna responded.

"I know you have a million questions, but don't ask them right now. Just smile and roll your eyes, and when you hang up, make up some big joke about what a lightweight I am. I'll call you to fill you in later, I promise. Now say, 'I hope you feel better.'"

Jenna did so.

"That was perfect. I'll talk to you later. And thanks for covering. If I found what I think I found, we might have a new angle to look at in regards to Holly's murder."

CHAPTER 15

Tj thumbed through the photos as Kyle developed the film from the unprocessed role. These photos were different. They showed more intent, spanned over a number of days, and all featured Holly.

The first photo was of her standing in the hallway of the high school, looking at something in the distance. There were several others of her at various locations around the campus. Tj gasped when she came across a photo that showed Holly staring at Jessie and Nathan as they made out under the bleachers the day before homecoming. Tj hadn't been aware there was anyone else in the area, but someone had to have been around to take the photo.

"These photos are different from the ones taken with the disposable cameras," Kyle observed. "Not only is the subject matter different, but it's from a 35mm camera, and based on the images, I'd say a telephoto lens was used in at least some of the photos."

"Someone was spying on Holly."

"It appears that way," Kyle said.

Tj continued to thumb through the photos. There was

one of Holly and Jessie talking alone in a den. Based on the clothes they were wearing, it was taken on the night of the party."

"The photos from the party were taken from the interior of the house," Tj realized, "which means whoever took them was with us."

"Do you remember anyone with a real camera as opposed to a disposable?" Kyle asked.

People had been snapping photos all night. She had no reason to notice what type of camera anyone was using. She didn't remember being focused on the flashes of light going off around her at all.

"No," she said. "I don't remember who had what type of camera."

After studying the photos, Tj was able to verify that Coach Fremont *had* been at the party, at least for a short period of time.

She focused on the photo of him staring at someone beyond the camera, but she couldn't figure out what or who it was he was looking at. The more she concentrated on the photos, the more certain she was that she had seen him at the party that evening but simply hadn't remembered it until now.

"Look at this one." Kyle passed a photo to Tj.

It was a photo of Coach Fremont and Holly. They were alone in what looked like one of the bedrooms in Brett's house. It was taken at an odd angle, perhaps from outside the window. While you couldn't see the actual image of either subject, you could see their reflection in the bedroom mirror.

"Oh God, I remember this. I walked in on them. It was..." Tj paused. "Horrifying. Coach Fremont had his hands all over

Holly and she looked like she wanted to puke, but when I started to enter the room to help her she waved me away. How could I have forgotten that?"

"You were drunk and it was disturbing. You must've repressed it," Kyle suggested.

Tj frowned. "I guess."

"Do you think the coach killed Holly?" Kyle asked.

"I don't know. Maybe." Tj furrowed her brow. "I can't figure out why she was letting him do what he was doing to her. It doesn't make any sense. I could have stopped him but it was obvious by the look on her face that she didn't want me to intervene. Holly wasn't the type to be a victim so I guess I convinced myself that her make out session with the coach was consensual. She certainly wasn't fighting him."

"Yet she ended up being the ultimate victim."

Kyle had a point.

"Do you think Holly and the coach had a thing going on?" Kyle asked.

"No. I can't even remember why I went upstairs. I do remember Holly and Coach Fremont were fully dressed; he just had his hands in inappropriate places. The coach's back was to me, so I only saw Holly's face. She looked like she was enduring and not enjoying the attention but she also made it clear that she wanted me to leave. I can't believe I forgot that."

Tj continued to stare at the photo. "Are there others?"

"A few."

Tj continued sorting as Kyle developed. There was a photo of Holly talking to Brett that caught her eye. They were outside near the split-rail fence that separated his parents' property from the forest. Holly had on the same clothes as at the party, so Tj had to assume the photo had been taken that same night.

"Look at this photo of Holly talking to Brett. It's dark, so it's hard to make out any details, but doesn't that look like an image of a person?" Tj pointed to a dark spot among the distant trees.

Kyle squinted. "I'm not sure. I'll scan the photo and then use my imaging software to see if I can enlarge and enhance the background."

There were several other photos of Holly in the background while Jada was talking to Nathan, and several of Holly sitting on the sofa next to Mia, who was talking to a guy Tj didn't recognize. She frowned as she tried to figure out who that guy was. He looked familiar, but as hard as she tried, Tj couldn't place him. He might have been new to the school that year. Tj knew most of the students who'd attended Serenity High, but there were a few students who'd transferred in for short periods of time who she never got to know. If Mia was talking to him, he was most likely from the drama or choir crowd. The more Tj thought about it the more certain she was that he was a new student to the school that year who had come with some of the guys from the football team. Tj texted Jenna a photo of the guy and asked her if she remembered who he was. Jenna was in drama club with Mia so chances are she'd have a name.

Mike Winkle. Jenna texted back. *Drama club member and friend of Teddy's.*

So he must have come with Teddy. Tj texted Teddy and asked if he remembered him being there but he didn't answer right away.

"I'm going to try calling Jada again," Tj decided as she

waited for Teddy's reply. "I don't know why she hasn't called me back, and I don't know if she knows anything, but if it's true Holly was blackmailing her, maybe she can point us in the right direction."

Tj called Jada while Kyle continued to work on the computer. If anyone could clean up the image so that it could be identified it was Kyle.

"Hey, Jada; it's Tj," Tj greeted when Jada answered.

"Tj, how are you? I'm so sorry I haven't called you back. I'm afraid I've had a crisis at work that has been demanding all of my attention this week."

"I'm sorry. Did you fix your problem?"

"Yes, thankfully. One of my larger clients had a problem with a hacker who kept me in a cat and mouse game for days. I think I caught the guy though. Are you at the game?"

"Actually, I'm not. I got tied up, but I hope to make it to the dance tonight. I'm sorry you weren't able to come."

Jada sighed. "On one hand I was fortunate I was here. If I'd been at Paradise Lake when the hacking thing occurred, it would have been a mess. On the other hand, I never should have let the *Second Look* lady get under my skin. When you have a secret you've been guarding for so long, you find you become very defensive about anyone poking around too closely. I know the fact that I cheated on a couple of tests in high school is completely irrelevant now, but making sure no one *ever* found out what I'd done was so totally engrained in my mind that I went a little nuts when that woman started probing."

"Ms. Colton seemed to think Holly found out you had cheated and blackmailed you into hacking into some student accounts."

"It's true," Jada admitted with a sigh. "I've regretted my decision to do what she asked every minute since then, but at the time I was really scared that I'd not only flunk my classes but I would lose my scholarship. I did what Holly asked to keep her quiet."

"Do you mind telling me whose accounts you hacked in to, and what Holly did with the information?"

"Holly wanted access to email records for Mackenzie Paulson and Mr. Hanover. I guess they had a thing going on and Holly wanted to find proof."

"Mackenzie was sleeping with the math teacher?"

"I'm afraid so. Looking back, it isn't as odd as it seems. Mackenzie was seventeen and Mr. Hanover was only twenty-four. The age difference wasn't all that huge, yet it was still illegal and against school policy. Mr. Hanover would have lost his job for sure and might very well have been arrested, and Mackenzie might have lost the role of valedictorian and the scholarship that came with it. They were both motivated to keep their relationship a secret, so they did as Holly asked."

"What did Holly want?" Tj asked.

"She wanted Mr. Hanover to fix her grades so she was getting a B or higher in all her classes."

"And Mackenzie?"

"Honestly, I'm not sure what she wanted from her. I guess you can ask her. Like me, I doubt her indiscretion in high school will make much of a difference to her life now. Of course Mr. Hanover still teaches at the high school, and he's married with children, so I suppose he has more to lose."

"Wow, that's a lot to take in. I appreciate you being straight with me."

"I've heard about the cases you helped solve. I think after all these years it's time to figure out who killed Holly. I loathed her when she was alive, and she really did hurt a lot of people, but she didn't deserve to die the way she did."

"I'll admit Ms. Colton opened Pandora's box when she started snooping around. I can't imagine how intense things might have gotten had she lived."

"Ms. Colton is dead?"

"Yes, she was killed in a car accident a few days ago."

"I hadn't heard. I wasn't happy she was snooping around, but I'm sorry to hear she was killed. Do they know what happened?"

"Not really. She was out on Old Sawmill Road at night during a crazy storm. They suspect she misjudged the road in the unfamiliar area."

"Sounds suspicious."

Tj wasn't about to disagree. She talked to Jada for a few more minutes before hanging up.

"Well that was interesting," Tj commented.

"Interesting how?" Kyle asked.

"It seems that the smartest girl in school cheated on her midterm exams and the most straight-laced girl in school was sleeping with the math teacher."

Kyle laughed. "I guess it happens. Do either of these events play into Holly's murder?"

Tj frowned. "I don't know. I do know that Jim Hanover is a new suspect in my book. If he was sleeping with Mackenzie, which in all fairness I still need to verify, and Holly was blackmailing both Mackenzie and Jim Hanover, it makes them equally suspect in my book. I didn't see Jim at the game, although I wasn't looking for him. But, to be honest, given what I know about him I don't think he'd show up."

"Do you have his phone number?"

"No. But I do have access to the staff directory which has everyone's address and phone number. Can I use your computer real fast?"

"Sure."

Tj logged on to the school site and pulled up Jim Hanover's personal information. "Oh my God." She turned and looked at Kyle. "Jim Hanover lives in a house off Old Sawmill Road."

"So?" Kyle asked.

"Samantha Colton was killed while driving on that road. My guess is that Colton was on her way out to speak to Jim when the accident occurred. The question remains whether her accident was really an accident. If Jim knew she was on her way to speak to him, it would have been easy for him to cause her to veer off the road at an opportune time."

"You think Jim killed Samantha Colton?"

"He had motive to if she found out what he'd done. It all makes sense. At first I couldn't understand why Mackenzie was second on her list. Although, if Colton did know about Jim and Mackenzie why wasn't he on her list?"

"Maybe when Colton made the list she only knew that Holly was blackmailing Mackenzie but she didn't know why. Maybe she found out later which is why she was going to talk to Jim but she never had a chance to update her list."

"Sounds like about as good an explanation as any. And if Jim knew or even just suspected that Colton knew about the affair, that would give him a good motive to want her silenced. I'm not sure exactly what the consequences would be at this point, but at the very least if the affair was made public it would have a negative effect on his family. He might even lose his job."

"Do you think he also killed Holly to keep her quiet?" Kyle asked.

"I think he very well might have. I'm going to go and talk to him."

"If he is guilty of killing Colton and/or Holly talking to him could be dangerous. I'm going to suggest that you call Roy and let him handle it."

"Jim won't come clean to Roy and Roy doesn't know him the way I do. If Jim lies to me, I'll be able to tell."

"How will you be able to tell?"

"I've played poker with the man on many occasions. His left eye twitches every time he tries to bluff."

"So tell Roy about the twitch."

"You have to know what to look for. If Jim is guilty I'll know it. If he's not, we can eliminate him from the suspect list."

Kyle pulled Tj close and looked her directly in the eye. "I know you want to solve this case and I know you think that you can handle Jim but I'm going to ask you as a friend who cares about you to please let Roy handle it."

Tj sighed. "Okay. We'll do it your way. For now."

CHAPTER 16

Tj called Roy to fill him in. After she'd explained about the photos as well as her conversation with Jada, he promised to track Jim down to have a chat with him. Tj figured that short of defying Kyle's wishes and going to see Jim herself, she'd done what she could. Of course now that she'd turned things over to Roy she felt antsy and at loose ends. Waiting for someone else to take action was not her strong point.

She texted Jenna to find out how the game was going. Jenna responded that it was all tied up and turning out to be the game of the decade. Of course the one game she had to miss would be the one everyone would talk about for years to come. Now that she'd passed the reins to Roy for the time being, she found herself wishing she'd stayed at the game.

"Since we are waiting for the software to finish cleaning up the photos do you mind running me out to the resort to pick up my car? I'll come back here with you to look at the photos, which hopefully will be done processing by then, but unless we find something significant, I think I'll head over to the school and meet up with the others when we are done here."

"Let me grab my keys."

Kyle dropped Tj at the house so that Tj could grab a sweatshirt which she figured she'd need once the sun set and then returned to home to finish cleaning up the photos. She decided to take a minute to let the dogs out since she wasn't sure when everyone else would return. She was just locking up when Roy called.

"Jim verified that Samantha Colton was on her way to speak to him when she had the car accident," Roy informed her. "I asked him about the blocked number and he verified that his home number is blocked so that he doesn't have students calling him at home."

"So if he was the one Samantha was on her way to interview he must be the one who caused the accident."

"If he did he's not admitting it. Not only did he deny any involvement in the accident, but he was adamant about the fact that he did not have a relationship with Mackenzie Paulson."

"Why would Jada lie?"

"I don't know the answer to that, but he definitely isn't admitting to the affair. We'll need to speak to Ms. Paulson and see what she has to say about it. Right now it's simply Ms. Jenkins's word against Jim's."

"Mackenzie was at the game when I left. I'll see if I can track her down," Tj offered. "I don't suppose Jim confessed to killing Holly?"

Roy laughed. "Hardly. In fact, he went so far as to accuse me of harassment for even suggesting such a thing."

"Yeah, I didn't think it was going to be that easy. Getting Mackenzie to admit to something as deeply personal as having an affair with a teacher is going to be tricky. I'll talk to her friend to friend and try to convince her that it is the right thing to do. If I can get her to talk I'll let you know and you can take it from there. I hear we're missing a heck of a game."

Roy groaned. "I heard the same thing. I was hoping Jim would be at the game so I'd have an excuse to head over there."

"You and me both. I'll call you back after I talk to Mac."

Tj tried Mackenzie's cell but she didn't pick up, so she texted Jenna to ask her to have Mackenzie call her. Jenna texted back to say Mackenzie had left a few minutes earlier after receiving a text and hadn't returned. Tj decided to check to see if Mackenzie had returned to the resort. She texted Kyle and let him know what was going on and then headed toward the cabin assigned to Mackenzie.

Unfortunately, Mac wasn't there so she tried texting her. Kyle called while she was waiting for a reply.

"So what'd you find out?" Kyle asked.

Tj filled Kyle in on her conversation with Roy.

"Did you happen to ask Jada if she found any proof the affair really happened?" Kyle asked. "She might have saved a copy of the files she downloaded."

"That's true. I'll call her back."

Jada hadn't saved any of the files she'd provided to Holly. She hadn't wanted anything to come back around to her. She did confirm that she'd read the emails, and there was no doubt in her mind the affair had really happened.

"You don't think Mackenzie is in any danger, do you?" Tj said to Kyle after she hung up with Jada and called Kyle back once again.

Kyle frowned. "Do you?"

"I don't know. If Holly and Samantha are dead and Jada didn't keep a record of the emails she discovered, Mackenzie would be the only threat to Jim. If he was motivated enough to kill twice to keep this quiet, it stands to reason he might do the same to Mackenzie."

"We don't know for sure that Jim killed Holly or Samantha," Kyle pointed out.

"True, but something doesn't feel right."

"It looks like the photos are almost done processing. Maybe we'll get a new clue."

"Okay, I'm heading back over to your place. I'll be there in a few minutes."

Tj climbed into her car and was heading down the drive when she received a text from Mackenzie. Apparently Mackenzie had gone to talk to Jim but her car had broken down on Old Sawmill road and she wondered if Tj could pick her up. Tj texted back that she was on her way before texting Kyle once again to let him know that she'd be later arriving at his place than she expected.

Tj heard her phone ding repeatedly as she drove indicating that she'd received a slew of texts, which she decided could wait until she pulled over to help Mackenzie. Sure enough Mac's car was on the side of the road with the flashers on. Tj pulled over and got out of her car. She walked toward Mackenzie's car which had the hood up limiting her view of the passenger area.

"This isn't the best place to break down," Tj said to Mackenzie who was sitting in the driver's seat. When Mac didn't respond she poked her head in through the window to find Jim sitting in the back seat with a gun to Mackenzie's back.

"I knew you were lying," Tj said to Jim after he directed her to get into the passenger seat next to Mackenzie.

"You should have kept your nose out of what was clearly none of your business."

Tj glanced at Mackenzie who looked terrified. She supposed she should be terrified as well but the emotion she was dealing with at the moment was rage.

"Toss your phone out the window," Jim instructed Tj.

Tj hesitated.

"Do it." Jim pointed the gun at Mac's head.

Tj tossed her phone out the open window.

"Start the car and pull onto the road," Jim instructed Mackenzie who did as she was asked.

"What are you going to do with us?" Tj asked.

"I really have no idea. Take a left on the dirt road that is just around the bend."

"You're only making things worse," Tj commented.

"Trust me things can't get any worse. Now be quiet so I can think."

The road that Jim instructed Mackenzie to turn onto was really no more than an overgrown logging road which made for a rough ride.

Tj held onto the dash as the car hit a rut. She glanced at Mackenzie who was as white as a sheet. Tj had been held at gunpoint a time or two in the past but she bet this was a first for her terrified friend. She figured she needed to divert his attention from Mackenzie to herself until she figured out what to do.

"Shooting a couple of unarmed women is really a cowardly thing to do." Tj challenged.

"Shut up." Jim pointed the gun directly at Tj's head.

"Let Tj go," Mackenzie cried. "This is between you and me. She has nothing to do with this."

"I wish I could." Jim sounded sincere. "But I have too much to lose here."

"I won't tell anyone. I promise," Mackenzie assured him.

"That's not what you said an hour ago."

"I know what I said. I was angry, so I wasn't thinking clearly. Let's just say I've had time to think things through."

Jim grunted.

"What are you going to do? Kill us?" Tj demanded.

"Not directly."

Tj had no idea what that meant, but she'd have to accept it for now.

Jim directed Mac to follow the narrow road which wound its way up the mountain. When they got to a spot where the road was blocked by a huge rock formation he told her to pull over.

He instructed both Tj and Mackenzie to get out of the vehicle. He tied their hands behind them and then tied them to a tree.

"What are you going to do, just leave us here until we starve to death?" Tj asked.

"I doubt you'll make it long enough to starve to death," Jim answered. "There's a big mama cougar that lives up in those rocks. I've seen her when I've been out this way hunting."

"Hunting in this area is illegal," Tj pointed out.

"That's the point you want to make?" Jim asked. "Look I wish I didn't have to do things this way, but you forced my hand."

"Please Jim," Mackenzie cried. "Don't do this. I said I wouldn't tell and I won't. Please."

Jim just laughed. "Who knows, maybe some hikers will

find you before the cougar does," Jim turned to head back to Mac's car. "But I doubt it."

"I'm sorry I got you into this," Mackenzie said after Jim drove away.

"Jim had a gun. You had no choice. Bringing us up here seems like a lot of trouble though, and the reality is, someone really might find us. I'm surprised he didn't just shoot us. It really would have been more efficient."

"Efficient?" Mac laughed. "You really are crazy. We've been tied to a tree and left as kitty kibble and all you can say is that our killer isn't efficient?"

Tj looked around. "Don't get me wrong, I'm less than thrilled with the way things are going but I've learned that it doesn't pay to freak out. Maybe we can get these ropes loose before Jim realizes that shooting us was really the better option."

"Jim won't come back and shoot us. He can't stand the sight of blood. I mean really can't stand it. He passed out once when I cut my finger while making us breakfast."

"He didn't seem to mind getting a little blood on his hands when he killed Holly," Tj pointed out.

"Jim didn't kill Holly."

"What?" Tj asked.

"He was with me the entire night she died. I came to the party looking for him, but he'd already left, so I went to his apartment. We were together until after sunrise."

"If Jim didn't kill Holly, why are we tied up and left for kitty food?"

"He doesn't want his wife and kids to find out he had an affair with a student, and he also doesn't want to lose his job."

"That's crazy."

"I couldn't agree more."

"So if Jim can't stand the sight of blood why did you let him bully you into texting me and driving us up here?"

Mackenzie frowned. "You make a good point. I guess I just panicked. I went up to Jim's to talk to him about the fact that, given the current investigation, things were bound to come out. I thought it best we take the initiative and tell Deputy Fisher about our affair before he found out on his own and used it as a reason to suspect us in Holly's murder. Jim didn't agree. He argued that I had nothing to lose at this point, but he had a lot to lose. I guess he had a point, but I was certain telling was the right thing to do. He pulled out a gun and threatened to shoot me if I didn't do as he said. I should've remembered he'd never use the gun, but having that thing shoved in my face completely shut down the part of my brain used for reason."

"That's okay. I get it. I was sort of freaked the first time I had a gun shoved in my face. Do you think he killed Samantha Colton?" Tj asked.

Mackenzie paused. Tj imagined she was considering her answer. "Maybe. He wouldn't have had to actually come into contact with her to run her off the road. She was coming over to interview him, and I know he was frantic to stop her because his wife was home. He texted me and said he needed to figure a way out of the impossible situation we found ourselves in. If I had to guess, I'd say he likely did run her off the road. Any luck working your hands loose?"

"I'm trying but Jim tied the ropes pretty tight."

Mackenzie nervously looked around. "Let's just hope it isn't feeding time."

"Yeah, let's hope."

There was a definite rustling in the bushes that Tj couldn't ignore. Hopefully, it was just squirrels or rabbits, but it wouldn't be unheard of for kitty cats to come looking for dinner at this time of day. Tj continued to talk as she and Mackenzie struggled to work the ropes. The sun would dip behind the mountain before long, and the biggest threat was going to be the cold rather than the cat on the mountain.

"If Jim didn't kill Holly, who do you think did?" Tj asked, more to get her mind off their predicament than because she really cared at that moment.

"I don't know. Holly made a lot of enemies. I don't think Jim and I were the only two she was blackmailing."

"What did she want from you?"

Mackenzie actually blushed. "She wanted me to fix the election for homecoming queen."

"I knew it."

"I didn't want to, and I was sorry that it affected you, but I really didn't want anyone to find out about Jim and me."

"Don't worry. I'm not mad. At least not at you."

"What's that?" Mackenzie whispered.

Tj squinted in an effort to locate the source of the sound they'd both heard. There was something coming toward them from the other side of the dense brush. Tj held her breath as she realized it was the mama cat and she was looking right at them.

"What should we do?" Mackenzie whispered.

"Just stay calm. Animals can sense fear."

"Calm? Are you kidding?"

"Hi, kitty. Where are your babies?" Tj said in a soothing voice.

The cat just looked at her.

"It might be a good thing we're tied to this tree," Tj said.

"Why?"

"If you weren't tied to the tree what would you do?"

"Run."

"Running is the worst thing you can do. The cougar will identify you as prey. Just stay calm and maintain eye contact with the cat. Oh, and try to look big. Or maybe that's just for bears. Maybe you're supposed to look dead for cougars."

"We're so gonna die."

Tj tried to figure out what she should do. The reality was, there wasn't a lot she *could* do. She tried to remember which behavior went with which type of wild animal. So far, the cat seemed more curious than anything, which was good, she supposed. The mama cat began to walk around the tree in a circle, but she didn't look particularly aggressive. Maybe she'd had a big lunch.

Tj had experienced run-ins with bears and coyotes in the past, but this was her first up close and personal experience with a cougar. She found she didn't care for the experience.

"What's that rumbling sound?" Mackenzie asked.

"It sounds like a car."

"Maybe Jim had second thoughts and is coming back for us."

Tj watched as Kyle's SUV pulled into sight. He honked his horn and the cat took off running.

"What have you managed to get yourself into this time?" he asked as he climbed out of the vehicle.

"What does it look like? Hurry up and untie us before mama kitty decides she's hungry after all. Oh, by the way, Kyle, this is Mackenzie; Mackenzie, Kyle."

"We met in the bar last night," Mackenzie reminded her.

"Oh, that's right. How did you find us anyway?"

"I slipped a tracking device into your pocket before I took you home to get your car." Kyle reached into her back pocket and pulled out a small chip. "See."

Tj let out a long sigh. "Why didn't you tell me what you were doing? It might have spared me some anxiety."

"Because you're tricky. You don't always do what's best for you. I didn't want to give you the opportunity to argue, so I didn't mention what I was doing."

Mackenzie laughed. "You guys sound like an old married couple."

Kyle freed Tj and Mackenzie, then offered to drive them both back to the resort.

"Can I use your phone to call Roy?" Tj asked him.

"Roy knows what's going on. I called him when I saw you had headed in this direction. He's already gone after Jim."

Tj leaned back against the seat and closed her eyes. God, she was tired. "Now all we have to do is figure out who killed Holly and we'll have this whole mystery package wrapped up."

"I think I may know that as well," Kyle said.

Tj opened her eyes.

"Who?" Mackenzie asked from the backseat.

"I managed to clean up the image of the shadow we saw in the trees enough to identify it as Nathan Fullerton."

"Nathan? Why would Nathan kill Holly?" Mackenzie asked.

"Have you read his work?"

"Sure," both Tj and Mackenzie answered.

"Do you remember his first book?" Kyle asked.

"*Obsession*," Mackenzie answered. "It was the book that made him a star."

"Do you remember the plot of the book?"

Tj's eyes widened. "Oh my God. He was writing about Holly."

"That's my theory."

In the book there was a teenage girl obsessed with a teenage boy who had no interest whatsoever in her. The girl tried everything she could think of to get the boy's attention, but no matter what he remained uninterested. The girl was used to getting her way, and she'd discovered along the way that the best way to get people to do what you wanted was to blackmail them, so she came up with a scheme to blackmail the boy of her dreams into loving her. But in the end he killed her.

"Nathan killed Holly because she was blackmailing him," Tj realized. "I had no idea that Holly was obsessed with Nathan."

"Chances are no one did which is why the connection to Nathan's book was never associated with Holly's murder," Mackenzie agreed.

"I think it also explains why he's kept a low profile. He came to Serenity early, so he was already here when Samantha Colton showed up. Everyone knew he was here and it would have looked odd if he left, so instead of leaving, he simply laid low in an attempt to avoid her. Once he found out she was dead, he realized it was safe to come out of hiding and attend the game. My guess is, had she not died, he would have made an excuse to go home without ever having made an appearance."

"This whole thing is so surreal," Mackenzie said. "I can't

believe Nathan would do such a thing, but I do remember him mentioning he had a stalker. At the time he said it in a joking sort of way, so I thought he was kidding."

"I wonder what Holly was blackmailing him with," Tj said.

"In the book, the obsessed girl found out that the object of her affections had been physically and sexually abused as a child," Kyle reminded them. "I don't know how close Nathan stuck to the truth in his fiction, so it could have been something else entirely."

"Wow," Tj said.

"Wow is right," Mackenzie agreed.

"Roy is going to bring Nathan in for questioning. Let's not forget that all we have at this point is a photo and a theory," Kyle said.

"I read *Obsession* a long time ago, but the more I think about it, the more convinced I am that the book is going to end up serving as a sort of confession," Tj mused. "It seems like every detail about the crime scene is exactly the same as the location where they found Holly's body. I can't believe I never put two and two together."

"I wonder why he wrote it all down and then had it published?" Mackenzie asked.

"Maybe he needed to confess but didn't want to go to prison. Writing a fictional account of the events was his way of doing that," Kyle said.

"I'm going to call Roy to ask him to come over once he tracks Jim down and talks to Nathan," Tj decided. "I need to find out exactly how this story ends."

"I thought you were going to the dance," Kyle reminded her as he turned onto the resort road.

"Honestly," Tj answered, "I'm way too exhausted. I bet Hunter will be tired as well after surgery. I guess I should ask him, but I think we'll skip it."

"That close encounter with the big cat took a lot out of me. I think I'll just head home," Mackenzie added.

"Don't go home early. Stay and have dinner with us," Tj said. "I'll order food from the Grill and we can relax on the deck of the cabin Hunter and I are staying in."

"I don't want to be a third wheel."

"You won't be a third wheel. Kyle is going to have dinner with us as well. Aren't you, Kyle?"

Kyle glanced at Mackenzie in the rearview mirror. "If you want to stay, I'd be happy to round things out."

Mackenzie smiled back at Kyle. "Okay. If you're sure."

Kyle grinned. "I'm sure."

CHAPTER 17

Halloween

"Trick or treat, smell my feet, give me something good to eat," Gracie said when Jenna answered the door.

"Don't you look beautiful!"

"I'm Cinderella." Gracie grinned. "Are Kristi and Kari ready?"

"They are. And we're all very excited about the Halloween sleepover."

Tj had invited Jenna and her girls to spend the night. Dennis had been called in to work when two firefighters from his department came down with food poisoning, and Hunter had decided to take Jake and his friend to San Francisco for a couple of days because Tj was going to be tied up. Ben went with Jake and Hunter to the city, and Mike was spending the evening with Rosalie.

"Kristi and I will be joining you after our party," Ashley announced in a very adult tone of voice. "There are going to be boys there."

"Kristi is very excited about the party and Kari is equally

excited to go trick-or-treating with Gracie. This is going to be the best Halloween ever." Jenna looked at Tj. "Is Kyle joining us?"

"Kyle is on a date. He and Mackenzie hit it off, so he's taking her to the Halloween Ball at Timberlake House."

"Awesome. It'll be just the girls. This is going to be so much fun," Jenna said.

"I'm in need of some girl time," Tj admitted. "I have snacks and soda for the kids to pig out on during the movie marathon Ashley has all lined up in the DVD player, as well as wine and cheese for the adults."

"Sounds perfect. Let me get my coat and we'll paint the town black and orange."

The four girls were knocked out on the floor in the den by eleven o'clock that night. Curled up on the sofa by the fire, Tj and Jenna decided to take advantage of the quiet before going to bed.

"It looks like you have a permanent addition to the family," Jenna commented as Pumpkin wandered into the living room and plopped down next to Echo at Tj's feet.

"It looks like. I wasn't sure another pet was the best idea, but Gracie loves Pumpkin and it seems obvious the feeling is mutual. She's really a well-behaved little pup."

"Plus she's adorable," Jenna added.

"There is that as well." Tj yawned. "I can't believe it's only been five days since we found her. What a week. It seems more like a month has gone by."

"It has been a long week," Jenna agreed. "I still can't believe Nathan killed Holly."

"What I can't believe is that he up and confessed when Roy brought him in for questioning. All we had was a theory. It's doubtful Roy had enough to press charges."

"I think Nathan wanted to be held accountable for what he did," Jenna said. "That's most likely why he wrote out a confession and published it in a book. I bet he never imagined it would take ten years for someone to figure it out."

"And we most likely never would have if Samantha Colton hadn't decided to avenge her sister's death and find her killer," Tj added.

Tj looked at the fire as it snapped, crackled, and popped. The wood her dad had brought in was freshly chopped and still contained a lot of sap.

"I actually feel bad about the way things ended up," Jenna said. "I really like Nathan, and I'm not certain the whole thing was his fault. If the book parallels reality at all, Holly threatened to reveal some very personal and painful information about him. I think the poor guy felt trapped and took the only way he saw out."

"What's really funny about the whole thing is that if Dalton hadn't been as obsessed with Holly as she was with Nathan, he wouldn't have been running around taking photos of her. And without those photos we would never have seen the image of Nathan watching Holly."

Jenna took a sip of her wine. "Did Jim ever confess to killing Samantha Colton?"

"No, but they can hold him on the kidnapping and attempted murder charges while they look for evidence."

Cuervo jumped onto the sofa and made himself comfortable in Tj's lap. Of all the members of the Jensen family, he was the least thrilled with the addition of Pumpkin.

"I'm sorry our romantic weekend with our guys got waylaid, but this is nice," Jenna commented as she nibbled on a piece of cheese. "It's been a while since you and I had girl time."

"It really has. We should make a point of doing this more often. It doesn't seem that long ago when it was us having the sleepovers."

Jenna leaned over and picked up a book from the coffee table. "Is this our senior yearbook?"

"Yeah. Ashley found it when we were looking for the Halloween decorations. She wanted to look at it, so I brought it down."

Jenna opened the cover and thumbed through. "Oh my. Look at my hair. What was I thinking?"

Tj laughed at the photo. "I have to admit that wasn't your best look."

"I look ridiculous, but you look exactly the same."

"You can't do much with my crazy hair, so I don't even try. It's been the same since I was a kid and will probably be the same when I'm an old woman."

"Except instead of curly auburn hair you'll have curly white hair."

"True."

"I love this one of Dennis and me at our homecoming," Jenna said. "We look so happy. Who knew what was about to happen, or how it would affect our homecoming ten years later?"

Jenna continued to look through the photos from that long-ago night. Tj mostly had fond memories of her time in high school, but the night Holly died was a sadness that had stayed with her through the years.

"I don't see you and Hunter," Jenna commented.

"We were probably in the hall necking." Tj laughed.

Jenna frowned. She passed the book to Tj. "Look at this."

The photo was of Holly and her date, but she was clearly staring at Nathan, who was with his date off to the side, and Dalton was in the background, staring at her.

"I've looked at this photo a million times and never noticed that," Tj admitted. "I guess you have to know what to look for in order to see it." Tj passed the book back and Jenna continued to thumb through it.

"I forgot you and Hunter were voted most likely to get married before our first reunion," Jenna commented.

"I guess that didn't work out as planned."

"Do you ever wonder how your life might be different if you had married Hunter right out of high school?" Jenna asked.

"I've thought about it from time to time," Tj said, "but I don't spend a lot of time agonizing over it. Part of me wishes we didn't have the years apart and the reason for them lingering between us, but I'm happy with my life. Hunter's mom was so controlling and I was so young. If we'd married right out of high school, she would have walked all over me. I think things turned out the way they were supposed to."

Jenna smiled. "I'm glad you've made peace with the past, and I'm glad you and Hunter are back together. He's a good guy."

"Yeah. He is." Yet Tj couldn't quite shake a slight feeling of melancholy.

"Something wrong?" Jenna asked.

"No not wrong. It's just that." Tj looked at Jenna. "It's nothing."

"Seems like something."

"It's just that," Tj paused. "I've been thinking about my relationship with Hunter ever since Jake convinced me to take a chance and make more of a commitment to our future."

"Yeah. I know that you were hesitant after what happened the last time you made a commitment to Hunter, but it seems like you are both in a really good place now."

"We are. He's been so good to me and the girls really love him, which is important to me. He really fits into my family and I know Jake will be over the moon happy if we marry and give him great grandchildren."

"What is it that you are trying very hard not to say?" Jenna asked.

"Sometimes I wonder if that is enough. I wonder if the fact that the girls love Hunter and our marrying would make Jake happy, is reason enough to marry."

"Do you love Hunter?"

"Of course. I have always loved Hunter. Even when he dumped me. It's just that..." Tj looked off into the distance. "Forget it. I've had too much wine tonight. It's made me all maudlin."

"Is there someone else?"

"Of course not."

"Kyle?"

"Of course not. Kyle is like a brother to me. I love him, but not in that way, and I'm certain he feels the same way about me."

Jenna didn't say anything, but she didn't look convinced.

"Hand me that bowl of candy." Tj decided it was well past time to change the subject. Jenna handed it to her and she picked out a candy bar. "I know I've eaten a million of these things already, but Halloween is the only night you can eat candy and the calories don't count."

Jenna glanced at the clock. "We still have a few more minutes before the stroke of midnight, when we turn into mere mortals unable to digest ten pounds of candy in a single sitting."

"Are there any more Milky Ways?"

"No I think the girls ate all the Milky Ways," Jenna answered. "Do you remember that Halloween slumber party when we were in the seventh grade?" Jenna asked. "I was sick for a week from all the candy I ate."

"Or the scavenger hunt when we were freshman?" Tj laughed. "We tried to be sneaky and try out a new neighborhood so we could beat the guys and we ended up on the other side of the river and couldn't remember where the bridge was to get back."

"We really did have a lot of fun." Jenna took Tj's hand in hers.

"Yeah." Tj squeezed Jenna's hand. "We did."

"Did we wake you up, sweet pea?" Tj asked Gracie, who had just wandered into the living room.

"I couldn't find Pumpkin." Gracie pushed Cuervo aside and crawled into Tj's lap. Cuervo settled in next to Tj's leg, and she pulled a quilt over all three of them, cuddling Gracie to her chest.

"I don't think Pumpkin liked sleeping on the floor where she had four little girls kicking her every time they rolled over," Tj said.

"Can me and Pumpkin sleep in my bed?"

"Absolutely."

Gracie started to doze off as Tj held her close.

"I love you to the moon and back," Tj whispered in her ear.

"I love you even farther," Gracie whispered back.

KATHI DALEY

Kathi Daley lives with her husband, kids, grandkids, and Bernese mountain dogs in beautiful Lake Tahoe. When she isn't writing, she likes to read (preferably at the beach or by the fire), cook (preferably something with chocolate or cheese), and garden (planting and planning, not weeding). She also enjoys spending time in the water, hiking, biking, and snowshoeing. Kathi uses the mountain setting in which she lives, along with the animals (wild and domestic) that share her home, as inspiration for her five cozy mystery series: Zoe Donovan, Whales and Tails Island, Tj Jensen, Sand and Sea Hawaiian, and Seacliff High Teen.

**The Tj Jensen Mystery Series
by Kathi Daley**

Henery Press Mystery Books

And finally, before you go...
Here are a few other mysteries
you might enjoy:

BOARD STIFF

Kendel Lynn

An Elliott Lisbon Mystery (#1)

As director of the Ballantyne Foundation on Sea Pine Island, SC, Elliott Lisbon scratches her detective itch by performing discreet inquiries for Foundation donors. Usually nothing more serious than retrieving a pilfered Pomeranian. Until Jane Hatting, Ballantyne board chair, is accused of murder. The Ballantyne's reputation tanks, Jane's headed to a jail cell, and Elliott's sexy ex is the new lieutenant in town.

Armed with moxie and her Mini Coop, Elliott uncovers a trail of blackmail schemes, gambling debts, illicit affairs, and investment scams. But the deeper she digs to clear Jane's name, the guiltier Jane looks. The closer she gets to the truth, the more treacherous her investigation becomes. With victims piling up faster than shells at a clambake, Elliott realizes she's next on the killer's list.

Available at booksellers nationwide and online

Visit www.henerypress.com for details

LOWCOUNTRY BOIL

Susan M. Boyer

A Liz Talbot Mystery (#1)

Private Investigator Liz Talbot is a modern Southern belle: she blesses hearts and takes names. She carries her Sig 9 in her Kate Spade handbag, and her golden retriever, Rhett, rides shotgun in her hybrid Escape. When her grandmother is murdered, Liz high-tails it back to her South Carolina island home to find the killer.

She's fit to be tied when her police-chief brother shuts her out of the investigation, so she opens her own. Then her long-dead best friend pops in and things really get complicated. When more folks start turning up dead in this small seaside town, Liz must use more than just her wits and charm to keep her family safe, chase down clues from the hereafter, and catch a psychopath before he catches her.

Available at booksellers nationwide and online

Visit www.henerypress.com for details

PILLOW STALK

Diane Vallere

A Madison Night Mystery (#1)

Interior Decorator Madison Night might look like a throwback to the sixties, but as business owner and landlord, she proves that independent women can have it all. But when a killer targets women dressed in her signature style—estate sale vintage to play up her resemblance to fave actress Doris Day—what makes her unique might make her dead.

The local detective connects the new crime to a twenty-year old cold case, and Madison's long-trusted contractor emerges as the leading suspect. As the body count piles up, Madison uncovers a Soviet spy, a campaign to destroy all Doris Day movies, and six minutes of film that will change her life forever.

Available at booksellers nationwide and online

Visit www.henerypress.com for details

Made in the USA
Monee, IL
17 August 2024